VANILLA VENGEANCE

BOOK ONE IN THE CUPCAKE CRIMES SERIES

MOLLY MAPLE

D1738007

MARY E. TWOMEY, LLC

VANILLA VENGEANCE

Book One in the Cupcake Crimes Series

By

Molly Maple

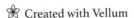 Created with Vellum

DEDICATION

To new beginnings,
And endings we put off for far too long.

Join Charlotte as she moves to Sweetwater Falls, only to discover that not even the sweetest of small towns are without their shadows.

"Vanilla Vengeance" is filled with layered clues and cozy moments, written by Molly Maple, which is a pen name for a USA Today bestselling author.

ABOUT VANILLA VENGEANCE

Charlotte McKay doesn't know what to expect when she moves in to take care of her elderly aunt.

When Charlotte discovers a dead body her first day in the cozy town of Sweetwater Falls, she worries she may have made the wrong choice, moving from the big city to a small town. She was hoping for a family feel and a fresh start, not a shakedown from local law enforcement and an aunt who keeps disappearing right when danger nears.

Sweetwater Falls is filled with loveable characters harboring dark secrets. Even though Charlotte is certain none of her new neighbors could possibly be the killer, she is beginning to learn that no one is above suspicion.

WELCOME TO SWEETWATER FALLS

I wasn't expecting to fit in with the small town of Sweetwater Falls on the first day, but I certainly didn't expect to stand out like a sore thumb. There seems to be a dress code that I did not know about before I packed up my pencil skirts and heels to move across the country. Everyone I spot on my drive into town is wearing jean shorts or overalls, while I look ready for a business meeting.

This town's décor looks straight out of the fifties. It's clean, for one thing, without the litter of cigarette butts or errant garbage blowing by. The trees all look uniformly trimmed. As I drive into the city, a breath escapes me that I didn't realize I'd been holding in.

I wonder how long it's been since I've waited to exhale.

Life was moving too fast for me in Chicago, and the bills were stacked sky high. It was good timing when my mother suggested a change of scenery for me. Great Aunt Winifred needs someone to look after her, and I am desperate for a rent-free place to live while I lick my big city wounds.

Sweetwater Falls: Population 5,682. Mom and Dad promised that Sweetwater Falls is ripe with family values and wholesome people, which doesn't sound bad at all.

I haven't seen my Great Aunt Winifred since I was a teenager. When I was little, I used to beg her to sing me to sleep with her cabaret voice. I never stopped loving the sound of her singing. She seemed old way back then. I can't imagine how ancient she must be now.

I check the address on my GPS again, chewing on my lower lip when it leads me to a white colonial with beautiful pale blue shutters. The east side of the house sports ivy-threaded trellises stretching from the garden all the way to the second story.

This doesn't look like the home of an elderly woman who needs help. The lawn is cared for, and the garden looks to be thriving. The house is on a sizeable plot of land that looks like it stretches a fair distance from the back of the home. The yard is dotted with bird baths, bird feeders, a garden bench and various other decorations that make the entire space feel welcoming.

A smile tugs at the corners of my mouth.

I like it here already.

"No wonder she didn't want to leave this place and go to a home," I say to myself under my breath. "It's beautiful."

I try not to let my eyes bug as I take in the rows of shrubbery, seeing the majesty that is a well-loved home.

"Okay, Charlotte," I say to myself. "This is your new start. You can do this." I'm sure my voice sounds forcefully chipper. It doesn't matter that I'm not all that experienced a caregiver. I am a fast learner.

Though, I'm not sure my stellar baking skills will translate to caregiving.

Still, Mom and Dad said that Aunt Winnie requested I come live with her. She must hold some faith that I will be good at this.

I tuck my purse under my arm and don my cheeriest grin. My heart is jumping with nerves that always come when I am starting a new adventure. But I don't let unquenchable trepidation stop my feet from connecting with the pavement.

The walkway looks like it has been swept, with no sign of leaves or errand weeds creeping onto the cement.

I was expecting the house to be in some sort of disarray. Perhaps she employs a groundskeeper. Mom and Dad made it sound like Aunt Winnie truly needed someone to look after her.

Maybe she will need indoor help—maneuvering with a walker or assistance bathing.

When I reach the front door, I raise my fist to knock, but before I can, the door flings open. A smile I haven't seen in years greets me. "Why, if it isn't Charlotte McKay. *The* Charlotte McKay. My talented grand-niece who bakes the best cupcakes in the world."

I nearly let my purse slip through my grip at the gregarious greeting. "Oh! Aunt Winifred, I didn't realize..."

I take in all five feet of her cuteness. I remember exactly her curly silver hair and rounded face with a smattering of wrinkles. Her glassy sea-green eyes never stop smiling, glinting with a joke only she knows.

I haven't seen her in at least a decade, yet she hasn't aged a day. "You look amazing!"

Aunt Winifred laughs like she always has—like a bubbling waterfall of pure soprano joy. "And you look like an angel that should be perched atop a Christmas tree. Golden blonde hair, just like your mother. Eyes bluer than a clear sky. And how tall are you now? Six feet?"

I grin at her gushing. It's not unlike the fawning she

did over me when I was a little girl. "Five-foot-ten, actually."

She claps her hands once, but doesn't invite me in. "Beautiful. And you arrived here just in time. I've got a meeting to go to, and the stinking doctor took my license away. You're driving."

Well, you are ninety-one.

"Uh, sure. That's no problem. Can I put my things in the house first?"

"No time. Let's just move in whatever we need so I have some leg room in your car."

I chew on my lower lip. "Okay." I don't mention that I have been in the car for the better part of two days, and could truly use a shower and some times to stretch my legs.

I do my best to grab multiple bags from the house, so at least I am partially unloaded.

After the second trip, Aunt Winnie stop me. "We'll be late if we don't hurry!" Aunt Winifred trots to my car, albeit with a slight limp. "We can unpack the rest when we get back. The meeting's already started!"

I want to take my time acclimating to the new home, but Aunt Winifred spins me around and all but shoves me back down the path.

Now that I think about it, she always was a little pushy. Though, it was never in a bad way. Aunt Winnie knows what needs to be done and sees to it with vigor. It's nice to know none of her spunk has faded over the years. When I was too nervous to flag down the ice cream man, she picked me up and put me on her shoulders so the driver couldn't miss me.

Aunt Winnie grabs up a knitting bag from the doorway and ambles after me, leaving the front door unlocked.

"Aunt Winifred, we should lock up. Do you have your keys?"

Aunt Winifred pauses and then scoffs with a smile in my direction. "You city folk with your jokes. What would I need to lock up for?"

I study her innocence with confusion. "Um, so no one steals your stuff?"

She looks back at her home curiously. "You're telling me I should worry about people stealing my collection of tea cozies? Or do you think they're after my wooden spoons?"

I narrow my eyes at her and tromp back to the house. "Do you have your keys?"

"No, so don't lock it. I'll never get back inside."

Part of me wants to laugh while the other part is itching to give her a lecture on safety. I take in her flippant nature which has clearly served her well and measure it against my careful steps.

I draw in a deep breath and try to get us on the same page. "Where are we going?"

"Town hall," she answers, waving for me to hurry along.

I was expecting to have time to unpack my things.

Well, if we're talking about what I was expecting, it certainly wasn't a woman so spry and lively, she doesn't seem to need my help in the slightest. If not for the limp, I would wonder why on earth I am here to help her. Mom made it sound like Winifred was in desperate need of assistance.

I open my car door for her and offer a hand to help usher her in, but she doesn't need it. "The meeting's already started! Hurry, honey cake!"

The corners of my mouth curve upward when her nickname for me when I was little sneaks back into my memory. "You could have given me five whole minutes to unpack the rest of my things from the trunk,'" I tease as when I slide into the driver's seat of my red sedan. "You don't want your honey cake turning sour on you."

Aunt Winifred laughs and claps her hands together once, which I think means we are off to a good start. She points a knobby finger toward the dirt road ahead. "That way until it ends, and then hang a right. If I miss the sheriff, I'll be sore about it for sure."

I start up the car, practically hearing my poor sedan

groan at being given so short a reprieve. Dirt roads make me nervous, so I take my time, making sure not to let my wheels succumb to the grossly uneven road.

"Is this the best this fancy car can do?" Aunt Winifred rubs her hands together like an evil genius readying for a speedy getaway. "I feel like we're in a movie. Two high-class girls looking for trouble."

I chuckle at her description of us. "I like that. What's your meeting about?" I hope my conversational diversion distracts her from my slow pace. I am not about to compromise my car after finally making the last payment two months ago.

"Flowers," she replies succinctly, rolling the window down. She smiles as the wind hits her cheeks.

I follow Aunt Winifred's directions, driving past oak trees that seem to stretch to Heaven, handmade quirky mailboxes in shapes of animals and tractors, a cornfield, and an old church with an actual steeple. When the road finally evens out and pavement glides beneath my car, my grip loosens and my speed picks up.

"Woo!" Aunt Winifred hoots. "That'll show the sheriff! Go, girl! Faster!"

Her glee worries me, so I search wildly for a speed limit sign. "Am I speeding?" My needle hits fifty miles per hour, drawing cheers from my great aunt in the next seat. Just in case, I slow down, taking the road at a more modest pace.

Aunt Winifred's smile falls. "You're a rule follower, I see. I've got my work cut out for me."

I snicker at her disapproval. "Is that a problem? I happen to like following the rules, especially ones that keep me from getting a speeding ticket."

My aunt puts her elbow on the ledge of the door, harrumphing that I have taken away her fun. "I guess that's one way to live. Your mother was right; you do need my help."

I guffaw at the notion that I came here for her to help me, instead of the other way around. Her moxie makes me chuckle, even if it's at my expense.

She points to the left, so I turn, eyeing a building that looks like a large red barn in the middle of older one-story commerce buildings. I spot a bank without a drive-thru option and a newsstand with an off-center sign that reads "Nosy Newsy". There is a diner that looks straight out of the fifties, complete with a jukebox that I spot, because I am driving at a modest thirty-five miles per hour. There are baskets of friendly white and yellow daisies dotting each business, some hanging and some planted in oblong boxes under the sills of wide windows.

"I think your town is doing a great job with your

flowers. I mean, look at how cheery that is." I point to a particularly lovely display that has tiny purple flowers scattered between the standard daisies. "Is the meeting about planting more? Because I vote yes."

Aunt Winifred motions to the big red barn, so I park in the lot behind it, next to a dozen pickup trucks. "Huh? No, no. We're not going to protest planting flowers. We are protesting the sheriff. He arrested Karen Newby. Can you believe that? We are demonstrating so he frees her."

I cut the engine and gape at Aunt Winifred. "I have so many questions. You said the meeting was about flowers. This is actually a protest? And who is Karen Newby? What did she get arrested for?"

Aunt Winifred picks up her knitting bag, her brow quirking as if I've said something daft. "The meeting is about Flowers. His name is Sheriff Flowers. And Karen is eighty-eight, and shouldn't be arrested for anything."

I only have more questions, but Aunt Winifred isn't having it. She pushes open her door, leaving me to follow haplessly behind. I don't want to involve myself in an anti-police demonstration before I've even unpacked my things in this town. I was hoping to blend in, join a local book club, get a quiet job at a coffee shop and enjoy a quiet life with my sweet aunt.

Angering the local law enforcement wasn't in my plans.

Yet here I am.

Aunt Winifred ambles quickly into the red barn, past a compost pen piled shoulder-high with a black tarp stretched across the lumpy top. The whole thing smells like rotten garbage and decaying meat. My nose twitches as I veer far away from it.

"Do you need a cane or something? A walker?" I ask, trying to be delicate about her wobbly gait.

Aunt Winnie's nose crinkles. "For what?"

I guess we're not talking about her limp. Maybe Mom will be more forthcoming about the kind of help Aunt Winifred needs.

When I enter the barn behind Winifred, I see at least three dozen people, all sitting in folding chairs facing the front. There on the foot-tall raised platform is a middle-aged woman with an angry, flushed face. She is gripping the podium with both hands. "We march today, and we don't stop until Sheriff Flowers knows he can't bully us into his prison! Do we want to live in a town where our cherished elderly citizens are locked up?"

"No!" everyone shouts in one voice.

"Then let's go out and make our voices heard!"

Apparently, the meeting is adjourned, because each person stands and moves toward the back exit, where Aunt Winifred and I just entered. They are holding homemade signs that are far lovelier than any I've seen at the protests in Chicago. Curly designs and painted flowers outline angry words that read "Release Karen, Lock up Flowers!" and things of that nature.

Yeah, I really don't want to involve myself in this protest, being that I know so little about the details.

I try to appear pleasant and unobtrusive, hoping to distance myself from any of the anger that seems to waft off the few dozen people emerging from the barn.

Winifred and I move into the sunshine and wait for the organizer to come out. Unfortunately, we are shunted right next to the compost pen. I breathe through my mouth as much as I am able, but the stench is so potent, I can practically taste the decay.

My nose has always been especially deft at picking out notes and details. In the kitchen, that's a gift. When standing next to a pile of rotting food, it's a curse.

I lean toward Winifred. "What did Karen get arrested for?"

"Shoplifting. Can you believe it?"

I can't help but ask the obvious. "She didn't do it, right?"

Winifred blinks at me as if I'm crazy. "Of course she did. Karen's got the stickiest fingers in town. Everyone knows that. But she's never been arrested for it. Sheriff Flowers is out of control. On a total power trip."

I balk at the logic. "So she stole and got caught, and

now she's being held accountable for it?" I lower my voice, knowing I'm not leaning toward the popular side. "Why are we protesting the sheriff doing his job?"

I can tell this is the wrong thing to say.

Winifred turns to face me, her frown fixed firmly on her face. "You don't understand, honey cake. That could be *me* locked up in there."

I guffaw at her. "Do you shoplift?"

"On occasion." She waves off my shock. "We always leave money in the spare change jar for whatever we take. It's all for fun. Keeps us young."

My brows furrow as I try to keep up. "So Karen stole something but paid for it by leaving money in the jar by the register? Why?"

"It's all part of the Live Forever Club. Karen, Agnes and I have no intention of fading quietly to our graves. We've got lots of living left to do. Spent too many years being good."

"I didn't realize being good was a bad thing."

"It is if you forget who you are along the way."

I let her words sizzle in my chest a moment before poking at them. "I can tell you love them—Agnes and Karen."

Winifred nods succinctly. "I do. They are my best friends. If one of us is in jail, the other two figure out how to get her out."

"That's oddly sweet."

Winifred chortles. "That's me: odd and sweet."

I have no idea what to do with this new information. I still feel as if I am catching up while people file out of the barn. They are all jovial and amped up, now that they are about to make their demands known.

"What exactly is the Live Forever Club?" I ask Winifred as she waves at her friends.

"Oh, nothing you'll need to worry about. You're not ready to join."

I chuckle at her moxie. "Is that so?"

She regards me with good-natured pity. "You're a rule follower." Then she reaches up to pat the top of my head. "That's okay. We can fix that in due time."

I mean, I guess it's true that I like following the rules, but it's never been looked on as a bad thing before. "You are something else, Aunt Winnie."

Winifred lifts up onto her toes and waves over a woman who looks to be around her age. "Over here, Agnes!"

"Winnie, I thought you'd deserted us! Thank goodness you're here, sugarbean. Without you, it wouldn't be a protest." The woman has short white hair, her curls pinned back to reveal a rounded face with pink cheeks to match her lipstick. She throws her arms around my aunt with gusto.

Agnes doesn't have Aunt Winnie's bubbly exuberance, but their smiles are the same—warm and welcoming without an ounce of judgment. Her green eyes dance with acceptance.

Aunt Winnie sifts her fingers through her shoulder-length silver curls, tossing her head back as her posture straightens. "I wouldn't have missed it. Don't you worry. Karen will be out of that cell in time for supper." My aunt keeps her arm looped through her friend's as she turns her to face me. "This is my great-niece, Charlotte McKay. She's staying with me. Charlotte, this is Agnes. She knitted my favorite scarf."

"Nice to meet you," I offer, extending my hand to her.

"Needs some looking after, this one?" Agnes asks Winifred, foregoing the handshake and going straight for a hug.

I love being hugged. It's not something I ask for often. Living on my own in Chicago didn't lend itself to many heartwarming moments. But as Agnes holds me close, part of my heart that felt unattached and drifting now slides into place. Perhaps affection is the thing I've been missing from my life.

I fight the urge to tell Agnes that actually, I am the one looking after my aunt. I'm twenty-eight years old, and haven't needed looking after since I graduated from culinary school.

Of course, I don't say that. I merely smile at what I hope is a joke.

Winifred nods seriously. "I worry we might be too late with this one. She's a rule follower."

Agnes closes her wrinkled eyelids as if my aunt has just announced I have contracted a deadly disease. Another hearty hug finds me, settling my soul in ways I never knew possible. "Don't you worry, dear. We'll set you right. You're in good hands with Winnie. If anyone understands life, it's her."

I haven't been hugged in ages. I try not to cling too desperately to this woman I am only just meeting, but my heart won't let go quite so easily. There is real love in her grip, and I feel it flowing into my body because she grants it freely.

I miss my mom.

I miss having real friends.

Life in Chicago was a busy bustle of trying to stay afloat while working a job that did nothing to satisfy the yearning of my heart. One bill after another began piling up, and soon enough, I found myself calling my mom, asking if I could come back to live at home.

Mom and Dad informed me that they are in the middle of putting my childhood home up for sale, but

Great Aunt Winifred was in need of a live-in helper, given her advancing years.

Though, as I look at Agnes and Winifred, I wonder if I am the one who is old and slow, and in need of help.

My rigid schedule didn't leave much time for hugs and girlfriends. Even though Agnes is probably triple my age, I can tell in an instant that I like her.

When she kisses my cheek, I decide on the spot that Agnes is my new favorite person. "You'll be okay, honey."

I fight the urge to confess how very not alright I feel. I left a life that never really felt like I lived it. Now I am heading into a new phase where I don't truly understand my purpose yet. I manage a modest, "Thank you. I think I needed that hug."

"Well, I've always got plenty." Agnes' head turns and she catches the eye of a woman who looks to be around my age. "That's my girl over there. You'll like her." She waves over the brunette, who has wide eyes and a sweet smile. "Marianne, this is Charlotte McKay, Winifred's girl."

I like my new label. Winifred's girl. It makes me feel part of the town. My aunt winks at me, and I can tell she is enjoying the sight of me mixing in with her friends.

Marianne is petite and peppy, with olive skin and her brown hair worn in two long braids. She smiles easily, and apparently doesn't believe in handshakes either. She's got a sign in her hand that's half as big as she is, glued to a yardstick. "So great to meet you!" she bubbles, keeping the sign in her fist as she throws her arms around me with surprising strength.

I giggle at the greeting as her sign bangs on the top of the compost pen behind me, and catches on the black tarp. "Nice to meet you, Marianne. Oh, I think you're stuck. Let me help."

She giggles as we untangle ourselves so I can turn and use my few superior inches of height to wobble the yardstick. I do my best to free her sign from the ratty edge of the tarp.

Agnes and Winifred laugh at us, because somehow, we only manage to get the sign stuck more as we wiggle it to one side, and then the other.

"I knew I would have a clumsy moment," Marianne frets with a self-flagellating smile. "The second I saw you were a cool city girl, I had a feeling I would make a fool of myself."

I chuckle at her assessment of me. I was anything but cool back in Chicago. I spent most of my time being invisible while in plain sight. "I think this qualifies as both of us sharing the clumsy moment, if you ask me. Almost got it."

I grit my teeth and twist the yardstick, hoping it will

untangle itself from the frayed edge of the tarp.

I grimace when all I manage to do is pull the whole cover down, which I know is going to set the stench free.

Miss Popular, indeed.

My nose crinkles as I finally manage to separate the tarp from Marianne's sign. "Here you go. It's..." But Marianne's expression is far from relieved.

Her eyes are impossibly bigger as she gapes up at the compost pile, pointing to the top. "Is that... Is that a human hand?"

I blanch as I turn, along with everyone else, and see what is indeed, a man's hand extended out from atop the compost.

One of the protestors screams so loud, my spine stiffens at the ear-piercing sound.

What was supposed to be a protest has instantly become a murder scene.

And I am standing right in front of it, holding the tarp like the girl caught with her hand in the cookie jar.

I try to shove the tarp behind my back, but it is clear I am the one who uncovered the dead body.

Just when I thought the worst thing in the world could be attending a protest of the sheriff on my first day in town, I realize I have stumbled upon something far worse.

Yes, I am blending in perfectly.

2

CRIME IN THE COMPOST

*N*o, no.

Maybe I am not seeing what my eyes are telling me is real and right in front of my face. A man's hand stretching out over a pile of compost that reaches taller than me isn't something my brain knows how to process.

Maybe I am seeing it wrong. I mean, perhaps we are all overreacting. The people around us are doing a dance of inching closer, then backing away, then inching closer again. Everyone wants to know who it is, but no one actually wants near the dead body.

I am standing near a dead body.

Revulsion, sadness and curiosity overwhelm me.

Winifred's eyes are huge with worry. "Is someone really dead up there?"

I can't imagine any other explanation, but that does seem the thing to confirm.

Since I am closest to the body, and it will affect me less because I won't know the person in question, I take it upon myself to investigate. I set my hands on the wooden pen and climb up so I can peer over the top.

Now I know why everyone is in shorts and overalls. My navy pencil skirt doesn't lend itself to climbing compost piles.

Still, I manage.

I cringe at the sight of a man, perhaps in his eighties, hefted high and in a clear state of decomposition. His wrinkled face and mustache are frozen in a forever frown, as if the man wore no other expression in his long life.

"Who is it?" Winifred calls up to me.

I turn my chin over my shoulder in her direction. "How would I know that?"

"Take a picture."

I grimace at the disrespect involved in that request.

Someone else calls for the same. There are various noises of assent that rise toward me, as if, because I'm tall and can climb a fence, I should automatically be the weirdo taking a picture of the dead body.

"Maybe someone should call the sheriff?" I suggest.

Aunt Winifred jabs her finger toward the top of the

pile. "Someone already did. Take a photo, honey cake. We want to know who's dead."

The nickname sinks into my chest, leveling my discomfort with a heavy dose of familial sweetness. I was always baking up new creations, so the family joke was that I smelled perpetually sweet, and came bearing desserts.

That's a far better reputation than "grown woman who takes pictures of dead people."

When I reach for my cell phone and slide it from my pocket, I realize that my family truly owns me. All my aunt has to do is fix me with a precious nickname, and I will do the unthinkable.

Plus, no one else seems willing or physically able to get up here on the ledge of the wooden pen, so I guess it is to me to identify the body before the cops get here. I can't bring myself to truly look to see if the photo is in focus or if I am getting the best angle. I just want to get away from the dead body and the ensuing stench.

I pocket my phone so I can climb down ungracefully, grateful to be away from the pungent odor. At this point, the stench feels stuck to my skin.

All at once, everyone starts talking.

"Let's see!"

"Hold on, Gretchen."

"Back up, Tom, she's my niece."

"Who is she?"

"Out of the way, you're stepping on my bum foot!"

I do my best to ignore the clatter of people, handing my phone instead to Aunt Winifred after opening the screen for her and sliding to the picture. "Do you know who this is?" Even though I've just been face to face with the deceased, I turn my chin in the opposite direction of the picture, so I don't have to see it all over again.

But the second Aunt Winifred lets out a bleat of distress, I'm jerking my attention in her direction. I reach out, hoping to steady her in case she feels faint at the sight.

Aunt Winifred pales, her mouth firming in a taught line. "I don't believe it." Then she looks up at me. "How could this have happened?"

I have no response, except to hold her hand.

Agnes looks over Winifred's shoulder at the picture. "Oh, my. Come, let's sit you down. You don't need to see that." Agnes takes the cell phone and hands it back to me.

I follow after the two. "I'm so sorry, Aunt Winifred. Let's get you out of here."

It's an effort, but Agnes, Marianne and I maneuver the growing crowd, who are all speaking in a dull murmur about the scandal that is...

...whoever this dead man is. I still have no idea.

I grip Winifred's elbow, supporting her as best I can while trying to distance myself as much as possible from the scene. I try to catch Marianne's eye to silently ask her who this man is, but she is fanning Aunt Winifred, so I'm left guessing still.

Winifred starts to cry, so I scramble for a tissue or anything that might be helpful. "I can't believe it. He had so much time left."

We lead her into the barn and sit her down. Agnes has tears sparking on her wrinkled cheeks as she sits beside her friend, her hand on Winifred's arm. "Not Gerald. It just can't be. We just saw him last…"

But Winifred puts her hand on Agnes' to still her words. She shakes her head while they cry together.

Marianne loops her arm through mine, keeping her voice hushed out of respect for the somber moment. "That was Gerald Forbine. He was courting your aunt."

I haven't heard the word "courting" in a long time, but it seems to suit this town well. I can picture my aunt sitting on the front porch, sipping sweet tea with…

I'll need to get a decent picture of Gerald so I can imagine him without the bloated features, orange hands and flies littering his body.

I cannot conceal my shudder, which sweet Marianne mistakes for emotion. She hugs me tight, even though I am a stranger. She knew the man, not me.

That's when it dawns on me that *I* should be hugging *her*, so I slip my arms around her dainty waist, offering comfort as much as I am able.

We sit together in somber silence until Agnes starts pouring out her heart. "He was so sweet. He brought you roses, Winnie. Roses with no thorns. Only a romantic does that."

Aunt Winifred nods, but doesn't add to the sharing time.

When the sound of commotion hits my ears, I stand and move to the barn door to see what has further developed. "The police are here. That's good."

Aunt Winnie stiffens, her eyes widening. "We should go."

"Go? Are you sure? Should we talk to the police?" I suggest, my hand on the door.

"Sheriff Flowers? Not a chance." When Aunt Winifred stands, I take her hand, making to lead her toward my car, but she pauses. "Actually, give me a minute. Stay here." Then she messes up her silver curls, making her look more on the edge of deranged when coupled with her reddened face and glassy eyes. To Agnes, she asks, "How do I look?"

Agnes gives her friend a thumbs-up. "Old. Do it, sister. I'll be your wing-girl."

I look to Marianne to see if she knows what they are talking about, but Marianne merely shrugs.

"You girls wait here. Actually, bring the car around and be ready to roll. Marianne and I walked, so we could use a ride home," Agnes tells us as she waves us toward the exit. "We'll be a minute behind you."

My mouth draws to the side with uncertainty. "Are you sure?"

Agnes' hands gesture more emphatically, practically shoving Marianne and me out the door ahead of them.

Everyone is crowding around the policeman, who looks to be in his sixties. He is in his blue uniform, his notepad out as he tries to write down what everyone is saying to him. To me, all the chatter sounds like a bunch of hysterics with no actual information.

Poor guy.

Moving through the crowd is slow going, but Marianne links her arm through mine. She herds me halfway through the mass of people. They are all clambering to give their two cents of who they think it is, and what they are sure must have happened.

True to their word, Winifred and Agnes follow behind, but they veer toward the police officer. I turn toward my aunt when her grief pushes her to throw her arms around the officer's waist while she blubbers into his shoulder. "Oh! I can't believe he's dead. What a world! I'll never be the same again."

"Oh, goodness!" Marianne tugs on my arm, making sure I see exactly how distraught our little old ladies are. "She hates Sheriff Flowers. She must be completely out of sorts to be leaning on him right now."

I nod, grateful I have someone next to me when this place has me completely thrown. "I need to get her back home."

"Agnes and I will help you."

I squeeze her hand in thanks.

I like Marianne. I can't help it. The wide eyes and long brown hair make her look like a cartoon princess, complete with an innocence to her higher-pitched voice. It makes me want to sweep the street in front of her, so she doesn't trip on an errant pebble.

My heart yanks in my chest as Agnes pries my aunt's hands from the officer's waist. The poor guy freezes, fumbling because clearly, he has no idea what to do when handed raw human emotion. "There, there, Winnie. Have you seen who it is? Can everyone just back on up? This is a crime scene now. You all need to leave so I can do some actual police work. Only stick around if you have useful information."

This, apparently, is the wrong thing to say. Every single person has their variation of a "Boot Sheriff

Flowers Out of Office" sign in one arm while throwing conjectures at the befuddled man as if they are actual facts. Everyone has an opinion. Everyone's two cents must be heard at that exact moment, before the man has even had a chance to identify the body.

Agnes helps Aunt Winifred through the crowd. While the two were barely upright on their way to the sheriff, they move surprisingly quick toward us.

"The car! The car!" Aunt Winifred scolds us.

Marianne and I are still standing around, trying to find a way to be helpful or supportive in Winifred's time of crisis. I forgot about bringing the car around for them.

Marianne and I spring to life, skittering into the parking lot like two naughty children caught sneaking out of bed in the night. I trot to my car and pull it around, getting out so I can help Aunt Winifred and Agnes into the backseat.

Their tears dry as if they were mere figments of my imagination. "Go! Go!" Aunt Winnie urges the second I get back behind the wheel.

"We'll get you home, Aunt Winifred. Don't worry." I turn onto the main road, pretty sure I am going the right way to get to her house, but Agnes directs me to go the other way. I comply, now completely turned around.

Even Marianne seems confused. "Where are we going, Agnes? I think we should get Winifred home."

But neither woman in the back is interested in our opinion. Instead, they feed me directions, devoid of all mourning. In fact, they look excited, as if we are going on a thirty-five mile an hour chase.

Agnes grips my headrest. "Is there any way you can speed up? We have to hurry!"

I point to the sign. "I'm going the speed limit. What's going on?"

Agnes only gives me directions, finally pointing me to the police station. My shoulders lower. "Oh. You want to report the crime and give your statement. That's good. But I'm sure Sheriff Flowers could have taken it just fine."

Winifred reaches around my seat and pats my shoulder. "This is better. Keep the car running."

I pull to the circular entrance of the rundown police station, which is missing the "r" in "Sweetwater Falls". I shrug to Marianne, who mirrors my actions. We stay put, because those are our explicit instructions given by Agnes and Winifred.

The two old friends amble at a brisk pace into the police station. Aunt Winnie's limp is visible even as she opens the door.

"They're acting weird, right?" I ask Marianne,

pointing to the women as they disappear into the building.

Marianne conjures up a mildly exasperated smile. "I've given up trying to keep up with them. The Live Forever Club does their own thing. I'm just lucky to be along for the ride."

I search for small talk, because I genuinely enjoy Marianne's company. "Agnes is your grandma?"

Marianne shakes her head. "My friend. We look after each other."

I tilt my head to the side. "I like that. Have you lived here long?"

"My whole life. Sweetwater Falls a good place to put down roots. I work at the library." She fixes me with a smug sidelong glance. "Head librarian," she says with her shoulders rolled back. I can tell she takes pride in her position.

I like her.

"Impressive. Must be nice, being in the quiet, surrounded by all that great literature."

She inhales with a precious happiness to her dainty features. "It really is. When there is nothing to do, I get to read to pass the time. It's Heaven." She turns in her seat to face me. "What do you do?"

"Well, nothing right now." I really hate saying that. "I was working at a restaurant in Chicago. I suppose I'll poke around later this week to see if there's anything available in Sweetwater Falls."

"Chicago? Sounds exciting."

"Meh. Exciting is another word for expensive. It was good timing for me to relocate." I thumb the steering wheel. "Know of any bakeries that are hiring?"

Marianne chews on her lower lip. "We have a diner, but there isn't a bakery. They do sell pies at the diner. That counts, right? That's baking."

My optimism begins to fall. "I guess I'll have to look for something else."

"For what it's worth, the diner is hiring for waitresses. Maybe you can start there and wait for a bakery to open up."

I can tell Marianne is trying to be helpful, but my spirits are starting to plummet. "I love to bake. Ever since I was little, coming up with new cupcake flavors was a fun way to pass the time. No bakery in Sweetwater Falls?" I shake my head. "It would be like a library with no books."

Marianne gasps at the scandal and places her hand atop mine. "I can't imagine how lost you must feel. We'll solve this. We'll find you a place to bake."

I am endeared to Marianne's plucky can-do attitude, even when the situation is clearly hopeless. "It's okay." I try to salvage our camaraderie and rescue it from the gray cloud that has passed over our introductions. "What is there to do for fun around here?"

"There's a drive-in movie theater."

I give a one-noted airy laugh through my nose. "No kidding. I didn't know those things were still around."

"Yep. We have events at the barn all the time, too. Dances, plays from the theater troupe, craft fairs, and things like that. Next month, there's a Twinkle Light Festival in the park." She presses her thumb to her chest, and I can tell she's proud of herself again by the way she gets this cute smirk. "I'm in charge of hanging the lights. Fifty-three thousand lights, and I get to be in charge of them all. It's a big job."

"Impressive." I share her smile because I can't not. "Do you need any help?"

Marianne bounces in her seat. "Really? That would be great. My volunteer list is a little thin. I mean, it's the Twinkle Light Festival. How could people not want to be part of making the magic happen?"

"Count me in. You tell me where to hang stuff and I'll, you know, hang stuff."

Marianne claps her hands. Even though she is probably my age, she looks like a teenager when she gets all giddy like this. We exchange phone numbers, and just like that, I have made my first real friend in Sweetwater Falls.

Murder aside, I like it here so far. I lived in Chicago for two years, and all I managed to acquire was debt. I'm in Sweetwater Falls for an hour, and I have already met my first friend.

I straighten in my seat when the door opens again. Winifred and Agnes come out, looking winded and gleeful beside a third little old lady who is cackling like a madwoman. "Who is that?"

Marianne covers her mouth. "Jiminy Cricket! They sprang Karen Newby."

Panic strikes my features. "What? The woman you all were protesting the sheriff over because she got arrested for shoplifting?"

Marianne snorts. "I know. Can you believe that?"

Though, something tells me Marianne (like Winifred) is more exasperated with the sheriff taking action than with Karen's actual criminal offense.

The back door pops open, and the three shuffle into the car. "Go! Go!" Winifred urges, shutting the door and banging on the back of my seat.

I peel out of the police station's circular drive. I follow their directions because to question them would give me more information that I am certain I don't want.

Marianne turns in her seat. "I can't believe you did that. How?"

Winifred laughs as she dangles a set of keys in the

air. "Old Sheriff Flowers isn't as smart as he thinks he is. Comforting a grieving woman can be dangerous business in this town."

I gasp at the scandal. "You didn't. Tell me you didn't steal the sheriff's keys!" Fear rushes through me at being part of something so illegal.

"It was a team effort," Agnes adds, frowning that she is devoid of credit for this criminal act.

Karen's cackle sets my teeth on edge. Her white hair is short. Her dentures are perhaps too wide for her thin and wiry face. "Wonderful! Drop me at home, please. I've got a library book that's overdue."

"No, you don't," Marianne says with a wink, holding her palm over her shoulder for Karen to high-five.

Sweetwater Falls is a strange place, that's for certain. But I can't dismiss the thrill that races through my veins as we drive down the dirt road, nor the smile that creeps onto my face at the jailbreak in which I just unwittingly participated.

I think I am going to like it here...

...If I don't get arrested first.

3

CUPCAKE THERAPY

*T*he last time I moved, I did all the packing and unpacking myself, which turned out to be whatever the opposite of a labor of love is. But with Marianne's help, the entire process is mostly done by the time Aunt Winifred changes into her pajamas. I still have to unpack a few boxes, but for the most part, I am moved in—officially a resident of Sweetwater Falls.

Aunt Winifred's house is clean. There isn't much clutter, other than her excessive penchant for doilies, which cover nearly every surface in the front room. It looks like a little old lady lives here. Judging by the mauve and cream décor, one would never guess that a prisoner-liberating, key-stealing woman lives here.

I should be tired, but I've got too much on my mind,

so I'm unnaturally wired as I pace the kitchen. "We broke a woman out of jail today," I say to Marianne.

She takes my cupcake pans out of a box and shelves them in the cupboards Aunt Winifred previously cleared out for me. "We did. You never know what's going to happen with the Live Forever Club. Last week, things got real bad with their poker night. When I came to pick up Agnes, Gerald and Amos Vandermuth were hollering at each other something fierce." She lifts her fist and imitates one of the old men with a baritone to her voice. "'You shorted me thirty quarters!' 'You're blind, Amos! The only shortening that's happened to you is because of your crooked spine.'"

I grimace. "Yikes. Sounds like Gerald and Amos needed to hug it out." It's partly a joke, but also partway sincere, being that these people are such huggers.

"Ho, no. Not those two. They're always finding something to argue about."

"You'd think two people who don't get along wouldn't play poker together."

Marianne blinks at me as if I've said something strange. "Of course they play cards together. They go every month. They're best friends." She shakes her head. "This is going to be hard for Amos, losing Gerald so suddenly. I'll stop by later this week to check on him."

I do not understand these people, but I do my best to

keep up with the town gossip. "I'm sorry to hear that. Losing your best friend must be horrible."

Not that I would know firsthand. I've never had a best friend before.

Marianne nods. "That, sure. But Amos is a real penny-pincher. I know they never settled up after that last poker match. Amos won't get his thirty quarters back. It's really going to eat at him."

"Are you serious?"

Marianne nods solemnly as she puts my spatulas and spoons into a drawer. "He's an odd duck."

"Seems that way. If someone close to me died, I would focus on the whole 'never seeing them again part,' rather than the fact that they owe me seven dollars and fifty cents."

My hands start to itch, as they always do when I know I'm about to be up all night baking. "Hand me that pan you just put away?"

"The muffin one?"

"Yeah. When my mind starts to work overtime, my hands can't help themselves. I have to bake something, or my brain gets stuck and I won't be able to sleep."

"That's a yummy way to process things." Marianne complies, and continues shelving my other items, handing me my mixing bowl when I request that, too. "When my mind gets overloaded, I usually eat all the ice cream in the house." She ducks her head, like she's confessing a dirty sin.

I cast a smile over my shoulder in her direction as I fish through the cupboards to see what ingredients I have to work with. "Feel like switching to cupcakes instead of ice cream?"

"Deal!" Marianne's grin is endearing, if not infectious.

I brought most of my own ingredients, but I am always looking for new inspiration, so I pilfer Winifred's spice rack. It gives my hands something to do while my brain shuffles through the facts as we know them. "So Gerald had a big argument about money with his best friend, and then dies a week later. That's something to think about."

I start by combining my dry ingredients, unpacking them from the box and adding them to a big bowl before putting them in the cupboards. The kitchen is yellow and cheerful, even in the middle of a conversation about a murder.

I pause. "We're sure it's a murder, right? I mean, he wasn't a farmer who... I don't know, forgot how to properly compost?"

Marianne snickers. "I don't think a body gets that high up by mistake. Yes to the murder, no to the farming angle. Gerald ran the Spaghetti Scarf."

At this, I pause. "Let me get this straight: Sweetwater Falls doesn't have a bakery, but it has an entire store dedicated to selling scarves and spaghetti? How does that even work? A boutique on one side and an Italian eatery on the other?"

Marianne shakes her head as if I've said something ridiculous. "No, no. It's just spaghetti. It hasn't been a scarf store since Gerald's mother died, like, back when I was a kid. He doesn't know a thing about scarves, so when his mother passed, he used the building to open up a spaghetti place. I guess it was cheaper to add 'Spaghetti' to the sign, rather than take 'Scarf' down, too."

I blink at Marianne, searching for a smirk or some sign that she's kidding, but she keeps unpacking as if nothing odd just popped out of her mouth.

Marianne sets the baking soda on a shelf in the cupboard. "Gerald's wife died probably a decade or so ago, and he kept the Spaghetti Scarf going. Kept true to her recipes, too. Makes me sad that he's gone."

"I'm so sorry, Marianne."

"Thanks. He never dated anyone in all that time, until last month when he took up with Winifred. I had high hopes for that relationship." She gives a long inhale and exhale, as if cleansing the grief from her soul as best she can.

I busy myself creaming the wet ingredients, taking my time with the strokes while I think through the information I have. "So it could have been Amos. Anyone else?"

Marianne shrugs. "No idea. Everyone in Sweetwater Falls is so nice. I can't believe anything nefarious would occur to anyone here." Her mouth pulls to the side. "I know Amos isn't exactly Mister Popular, but I like him. He helps me on occasion when I get stumped balancing the books for the library. I can't believe he would murder Gerald."

Marianne is certain, but given we just sprang a shoplifter from jail, and I uncovered a dead body my first day here, I am positive that Sweetwater Falls has a dark side.

4

TWO NIGHTS AGO

*A*unt Winifred wakes me with a kiss to my cheek. I startle, sitting up only to realize I fell asleep at the round kitchen table after my fourth batch of vanilla latte cupcakes came out of the oven. "Oh! Did I... Oh, man. I fell asleep down here."

"Never made it to your bedroom." Aunt Winifred pinches my cheek and then blows a puff of air at me, rattling particles of flour loose and scattering them atop the table. "Poor thing. You had a wild first day in Sweetwater Falls. You'll need your beauty sleep if you're going to keep up with us."

"No kidding." I feel awful. I have been little help to her at all. After I finished unpacking, I baked myself to sleep. It's not the first time I have done this, but it is the first time I had a murder on my mind that kept me from my down pillow.

I notice Winnie's limp as she goes to the coffee pot, which has been brewing for who knows how long. She pours me a cup of black coffee, which to me, is only something I drink under duress.

She is fully dressed and looks showered, complete with her makeup on as she sips from the mug she poured for herself.

I sit up more fully. "What time is it?"

"Nine in the morning. You sure do like to sleep in." Her head tilts to the side. "You want to talk about it, honey cake?"

I run my hand through my blonde curls, shaking some flour loose. "I should ask you the same question. It's your boyfriend who passed. Do you want to talk about it?"

Winifred sits down in the chair, repositioning a few times to accommodate her sore leg. "First off, a woman my age doesn't have boyfriends. I have gentlemen callers."

I dip my head in her direction. "Well, then I'm sorry you lost your gentleman caller. Was he a good guy?"

"He brought me roses," she replies wistfully. Then she straightens and waves off my concern. "But we had only just started dating last month. It was no torrid love affair. Still, I was the first woman he took out since his wife passed. It felt special to me, even if it was brief."

My eyebrows rise. "A decade is a long time not to date anyone." When Winifred looks surprised that I know this detail, I add, "Marianne mentioned last night that Gerald's wife died a decade ago."

"Yes, well, it's true. Gerald stayed single ten years to the day from when his wife passed. Ovarian cancer." She shudders. "Horrible thing to go that way. She was a good woman. A good friend." She takes another sip of her coffee. "He asked me out the day after the ten-year anniversary of her death, and I didn't hesitate." She looks down into her mug. "Maybe I should have." Then another thought chases in on the heels of that one. "No, no. No regrets. That's not how a member of the Live Forever Club acts. Dating Gerald was a good thing. We had a handful of happy dates before he passed."

My knee-jerk reaction is to delve deeper into her regret. Why should she be sad she dated him? "Sounds like he was a nice guy. What did you two do on your dates?"

Winifred smiles wistfully at me over her mug. "He took me to the drive-in. He's got an old car he was constantly tinkering with and wanted to show off. It was nice to feel all fancy and desired." She looks down into her coffee. "His palms were sweaty when he held my hand. It's been a long time since I've made a man's palms sweat."

I cast her a mischievous look as I stand and pull the frosting out of the fridge. The cupcakes were too hot to frost last night, but that didn't stop me from making an epic quadruple batch of butterscotch buttercream frosting. "I'm sure Sheriff Flowers is sweating plenty, now that his keys and his prisoner have gone missing."

Winifred sniggers into her mug as she takes another sip. I don't know how people can drink coffee with no sweetener.

I take a spoon from the drawer and scoop a dollop of my homemade frosting from the bowl and plop it into my coffee. I sit back down and give my beverage a stir.

Aunt Winifred recoils. "What did you just do?"

My neck shrinks as I stir the buttercream through the coffee. "I need my coffee to taste like a cavity, otherwise it's not worth it."

Winifred blanches. "You just ruined a perfectly good beverage, young lady."

I sip my newly improved coffee, and my whole body snuggles around the warmth. "Oh, that's good." I do my best baking when my mind is preoccupied, so I know this batch of cupcakes is going to be particularly amazing. If the frosting is any indication, I've hit a new high, while trudging through a personal low.

When the doorbell chimes, Aunt Winifred stands to answer.

I take my time sipping my hot beverage, enjoying the smack of sweetness that gives me a good reason to wake up. I am sure I look exactly as disheveled as I feel, but that's the least of my worries. I'm here for Winifred, so that's going to be my focus today.

After a shower.

I stand to go upstairs to my new bedroom, but the gruff sound of a man's voice pauses my steps.

"That's not what I came here to talk about, Winifred. I want to know your whereabouts three nights ago."

I tiptoe in bare feet toward the living room, noting how strange a police officer looks standing amid her lacy doilies that litter just about every surface in the mauve room. The antique furniture looks too fragile to sit on, so the police officer stands in the entryway, his lips taut with displeasure.

Winifred's flippant disregard of law enforcement is fascinating to watch. She waves him off dismissively, as if he is a fly meant to be swatted away. "Oh, none of your business. I was in my house, knitting a new doily. Want to see?"

Whatever level of pushover Sheriff Flowers usually is to this town, it is clear that a murder ups the stakes. His square jaw juts out at his dimpled chin. He runs his hand over it as he sighs, exasperated already. "I have it on good authority that you were with the recently deceased."

"You'll have to be more specific."

"Gerald, Winifred. I know you were with Gerald Forbine three nights ago. Someone reported they saw you two arguing."

I want to lunge forward and tell her not to say anything that could be damning, but I keep my strides measured so as not to seem too eager. I desperately want to stave off anything that might paint Aunt Winifred in a damning light. I stand beside her, my hand on her shoulder. "Who reported that?" I ask him, asserting myself where I am probably not welcome.

Winifred straightens now that I am enforcing her stalwart attitude. "Yeah, does this 'someone' have a name?"

Sheriff Flowers regards me with a dip of his chin. I can tell already that I am not his favorite person. "That's confidential. Protect the witness and all that."

Winifred raises her chin. "Then my nighttime whereabouts are also confidential."

The sheriff pulls a notepad and pen out of his pocket. "Is that your official statement?"

She pushes a fist to her hip. "It's my Broadway show-tune. Want to hear the chorus?"

I can tell this is going south real quick. I make to steer Winifred away from the living room, but she will not be moved.

"It goes a little something like this: 'Down with Flowers! Down with Flowers!'" Winifred punches her fist in the air, her soul filled with fire and coffee.

I steer my aunt out of the living room, excusing us as only one can do in a small town, dismissing the sheriff as if he is a schoolboy who has spoken out of turn.

"This isn't over, Winifred," the sheriff warns.

But it is for my great aunt. She leans on my arm and turns toward the kitchen, effectively shutting down the conversation.

Aunt Winnie's limp isn't as bad as it was yesterday, but it's still noticeable. I sit her down in a wooden chair at the table and press her mug into her palm. "It's going to be okay. He's gone now."

"Actually," the sheriff calls from the other room, and then invites himself into the kitchen, "I'm not finished yet. Winifred, I'm going to get some straight answers from you. None of this 'knitting doilies' nonsense. I know all about the Live Forever Club. I know everything that you old biddies get up to." He plops down in the seat I was occupying not five minutes ago and leans forward. "I know who sprang Karen Newby from my jail cell." He sets his notepad atop the table and presses his finger to the top. "So unless you want me to take you in for that, you'll start getting real cooperative real fast."

It's the only thing that sobers my aunt.

I swallow hard and move my coffee to the counter, pouring him a cup and setting it beside his notepad. Then I do my best to blend into the background while remaining present, in case Winifred needs me to intervene.

I take my time frosting my sixty vanilla latte cupcakes, moving as quiet as possible while still managing to get the rosettes piped with precision. No use putting in a half effort right at the finish line. Sure, the cupcakes would taste just fine if I blobbed the frosting on top, but I've never been satisfied with "just fine" cupcakes. If I care about something, I like to go all the way.

Aunt Winnie taps her finger on the tabletop. "Look, Flowers. My business is my business. If you want the details of my personal life, you have to be part of my life, not sniff around the outskirts whenever there's a scandal. That's not a friend."

The sheriff takes her chiding in stride. When he replies, his tone is less antagonistic. "I'm not here as a friend, Winifred. I'm here because someone saw you arguing with Gerald two nights before his body was discovered. What was the argument about?"

Aunt Winnie's chin firms. "He crochets better doilies than I do, and I was sore about it."

Man, this woman with her snark. Not even *I* buy that one.

The sheriff cocks his head to the side. "Winifred."

My aunt crosses her arms over her midsection. "He didn't want to go dancing."

"Winifred."

"We were rehearsing an argument from a play."

The sheriff sits back, and I can tell he is gearing up to play hardball.

As quick as I can without looking too eager to interfere, I slide a cupcake before him. I set another in front of my aunt. "You both get to be my taste testers. Let me know what you think."

"It's nine o'clock in the morning," the sheriff scolds me, though he unwraps the cupcake all the same.

It's a guilty pleasure of mine to watch people take the first bite of one of my cupcakes. True to form, Sheriff Flowers closes his eyes when the fluffy cake hits his tongue. A low "mm" noise escapes him, and for a second, he looks younger, like a boy enjoying a snack. He inhales deeply, and on his exhale, he opens his eyes with decidedly less aggression in them. "This is incredible, young lady. What flavor is that?"

"Vanilla latte cupcake with a butterscotch butter-cream. My own recipe."

"Well, it's the best I've ever had."

I always love hearing that. My spine lengthens as pride lifts my spirits. "Thank you. I'll pack a few up to send to the precinct." I get out a to-go box and set half a dozen inside, sealing it with the sticker that has my logo printed on it, back when I was determined to open up my own bakery.

Back when I had ambition, no bills, and about five fewer years on me.

Back when I was optimistic that life would gift me what I wanted in the form of a bakery all my own.

Aunt Winifred gives me a secret smile because she knows how much pride I take in my baking. I practiced in the kitchen with her when I was younger, baking up a storm and making a mess, while splotching flour hand-prints along every surface.

She takes a bite of hers, and the same reaction takes place. Even so, I watch it unfold as if it is a standing ovation. The closing of the eyes, the "mm" noise, the inhale followed by the contented exhale.

Every. Single. Time.

Never gets old.

The two pick up their back and forth with decidedly

less venom this time around as they munch on their cupcakes.

Sheriff Flowers takes a sip of his coffee. "Winifred, I want to catch who did this to Gerald. I know it wasn't you, but I need to do my due diligence. What were you arguing about? It might give me a clue that could lead me to the real killer."

There. That was much better.

I don't believe in magic. Not really. But I do know that nothing terrible exists in the world when a person eats one of my cupcakes. While they eat, I can see the tension lifting off of them, giving them over to become more amiable with each other.

Winifred sips her coffee and takes another bite. "I broke things off with Gerald, and he didn't understand why."

I can tell the sheriff is struggling to not ask her the reason for the breakup. Instead, he goes for empathy. "Sounds like it got heated."

"Well, not heated enough for me to kill him. Did you ever find out how the person did it?"

"Looks like an axe or some sort of long blade, straight to the sternum."

She lets a long breath in and out through her nose. "Well, feel free to check my axe for bits of my dead gentleman caller. I didn't kill him, and I don't know who did."

"What about his hands?" I ask, remembering the sight of his hands and forearms painted in an orange hue. "Did he have anything telling on him? That might point you in the right direction."

The sheriff frowns at me. "Nothing unusual."

I chew on my lower lip, holding back my protest that yes, his hands were stained orange. Why would Sheriff Flowers omit that detail? It seems like a clear clue. Not too many people walk around with orange painted on their limbs.

When he sees the hesitation playing out on my face, he doubles down. "What? His hands weren't holding anything damning. It's the big gash to the middle of his chest I'm concerned about."

"My mistake."

I know what I saw. Either Sheriff Flowers is terrible at his job, or he saw the orange staining on Gerald's hands and arms and is pretending it wasn't there.

The sheriff stands, jabbing his finger to the top of the table. His attitude is in full swing now that his cupcake has been devoured. "Don't leave town, Winifred. All signs point to you being the most likely killer. I'd hate to think of how few people would protest me putting away a murderer, no matter how well-liked you are in Sweetwater Falls."

My aunt puts up a brave front, but I can see the fear when she swallows hard, her eyes rounding with worry.

The sheriff is ignoring the oddity of the man's hands streaked with orange paint. He is shifting all the blame to my aunt.

Why?

Though I don't know yet what it means, my lips press together. I keep to myself that I think I may have stumbled upon my very first clue.

5

WAITRESS

*W*inifred needs me for precious little. She has a full schedule that has nothing to do with me.

I am not sure how I feel about this. I like being useful, and I was under the impression from my mother that Winifred needed a helper. To have her spry and energetic with direction and a lively social group? I hope I can be useful at all around here.

I vacuum and wash the dishes, then cast around for any other way I can be helpful.

When Aunt Winnie shoos me toward the door after finishing her morning dusting, I take her advice to heart. "Go enjoy the town. You need to get used to the sites."

Even though I am freshly showered and dressed in

my black skirt and a pink blouse, I worry that being away from the house is a bad idea. After all, the last time I went into town, I discovered a dead body.

"I dunno. Are you sure you don't need my help with anything? Mom made it sound like you needed me here, but I'm starting to think she was worrying too much."

Winifred sniggers as she fishes through her knitting bag. "Well, that always was your mother. She's not worried about my health. She knows I'm right as rain. She's more worried about the things I get up to. My behavior is 'not befitting a lady of my age,' I think were her exact words."

"So I came here to keep you out of jail?"

Winifred touches on the end of her nose. "Bingo. Bang-up job you're doing, too. I haven't been arrested once since you got here."

I mime an exasperated laugh, and then point to her leg. "What about your limp? I can tell it's an effort for you to get around. How can I help?"

Winifred narrows her eyes at me, and I know I have touched on a sore subject.

Tough. Pride doesn't matter as much as being healthy and safe.

"It's a little sore, but it'll heal up in a week or so." Winifred raises her hand without a hint of sass. "Honest. You're going to age prematurely, worrying about me like this. Go have fun. Something tells me your life before Sweetwater Falls wasn't filled with a whole lot of the stuff."

I swallow hard, knowing she couldn't be more right. "I suppose I could look for a job in town."

Winifred rolls her eyes at me, smiling with exasperation. "Well, that's one interpretation of 'go have fun.'"

"Where are you off to?"

She jangles a key ring. "I need to go drop the sheriff's keys in the parking lot of the precinct, so he thinks he had a clumsy moment and lost them."

I giggle airily through my nose. "You have a problem, Aunt Winifred."

"I'll take my problems over yours any day."

I guffaw at her good-natured jab. "Is that so?"

"My problems got my dear friend freed from jail and gave me a handful of fun nights with a lovely gentleman before he passed. Your problems are far more serious."

I cross my arms and tilt my hip to the side. "And just what is my problem?"

Winifred points to me with pity in her eyes. "You don't know how to have fun."

I gape at her, but when I make to argue, I realize I have no rebuttal.

I *don't* know how to have fun. I think big city life squashed that desire out of me altogether.

Winifred blows me a kiss and ambles out the front door. She steps into her golf cart, which I'm learning is how most of the elderly community in Sweetwater Falls gets around when they don't trust themselves behind the wheel of a car.

I take my time talking myself into getting into my red sedan. I spend even more time parked outside of Bill's Diner, convincing myself that this was a good idea. The neon sign is old. The "B" isn't lit, making it look like I am about to step into "ill's Diner".

Even before I step inside, I am convinced that the inside has not been updated in decades.

Maybe they will let me bake here. I cross my fingers and wish my most excellent wish that after they taste my cupcakes, they have to let me put some of my creations on the menu. It's a long shot, but I have to try. I don't want Sweetwater Falls to hold misery for me because I didn't give it my all.

I get my hopes too high, because I realize that the moment I set foot into the 1950s establishment, the only reason I want to work here is so I can use their massive ovens. There is no other reason why I would want to work here. I am four steps in, and my skin feels coated in fry oil. The tang of ketchup pricks my nose and the oldies station plays some whiny song about falling in love.

There are ten tables, five of which are occupied.

I don't want to wait tables, as Marianne suggested. I want to bake.

Please, let me bake.

When the teenaged hostess greets me with a lackluster "Table for one?" I offer up a pleasant smile.

"Actually, I was hoping to see if you had any job openings. Is there a manager I can speak to?"

The teenaged girl pops her pink gum and scratches a spot on her nose. "Um, sure. Bill?" She turns and raises her voice toward the kitchen. "Bill? Some city woman is here to see you."

Bill comes out with a towel in his hands, stopping short when he sees me. "We're up to code," he says, as if we are in the middle of some argument of which I am unaware. "I cleaned out the grill last night. No need for an inspection."

Bill is sweating at the sight of me. His mid-fifties skin is weathered and reddened from either the sun or too much time spent standing over the grill in the kitchen. He stands just over six feet tall, with long arms that seem disproportionate to his pooched torso.

I clutch the box of cupcakes in my hands, hoping they speak for me when I start to clam up. "I'm not a health inspector. I was hoping you might have a job opening. I'm new in town, and looking for work."

When my words start to sink in, Bill's bulbous nose scrunches. "What? You're sure you're not here for an inspection?"

"Pretty sure."

He motions to my clothes. "Then why are you dressed like that?"

I glance down at my black skirt and pink blouse. "Like I'm ready for a job interview?"

"Are you thinking we need someone to do our taxes? Because I do those on my own just fine."

I'm starting to feel more and more foolish as I shift my weight from one foot to the other. I hold my to-go box and pray I don't drop it. "I was hoping to work in the kitchen. Possibly as your baker."

His brows furrow, making one hairy line across his forehead, instead of the traditional two. "This is a diner, not a bakery. You got waitressing experience?"

"No, but I'm a fast learner."

Why? Why did I add that in? I don't want to be a waitress here. I want to bake. Why am I agreeing to a job I don't want?

Probably because I'm broke, I remind myself none too kindly.

"Fine. You can start as soon as you change out of that getup. My customers won't take well to your uppity attire."

My mouth draws to the side to hem in my stubborn rebuttal. My aim was to come in here and offer him a cupcake to audition for the role of a baker, but I keep the box closed. Clearly he has no interest or need for what I actually came here to do.

Why *did* I come here? I need a job, sure, but I want to come alive when I go to work, or at least not feel like I am slowly dying because I am so divided from my passion.

I want what Winifred has—friends she loves so much, she busts them out of jail. She has an active social life filled with intrigue. She has a home dotted with her passions.

I guess waiting tables will have to suffice for now, since this town lacks the one establishment I crave.

I lower my head. "Thank you, sir. Bill. I can start tomorrow." We hammer out a schedule and a pathetic hourly wage. Each detail makes my heart sink into my stomach.

This is not why I came here.

6

MY FAVORITE LIBRARIAN

*I*nstead of heading home, I take my dismal mood to the library, grateful to see Marianne's smile when I locate the help desk.

The building is beautiful—breathtaking, even. It looks like it was once a cathedral, complete with a steeple and vaulted ceilings. The stained-glass windows cast colorful designs on the polished floors. There is a dated look about the place, but that only adds to its charm.

Her posture straightens as she fixes me with her bright disposition. "Hey there, Charlotte. What brings you in today? Anything I can help you find?" She is wearing her brown hair in two long braids today.

I tap on the lid of my to-go box. "I actually came to

find you. I finished the cupcakes I started last night and thought you might like some."

Her eyes light up, growing impossibly rounder. "Oh, thank you! I knew this would be a good day, I just didn't know how. Now I know."

There isn't anyone around in the library, and she doesn't appear to be working on anything other than her worn copy of Wuthering Heights, so I don't feel terribly guilty taking up her time. "I got the job at Bill's Diner."

"Oh, that's great! You love baking." She pauses to lean forward, her voice dropping to a whisper. "And their pies are terrible."

"Not in the kitchen. I'll be waiting tables." It is clear by my glum demeanor that this is not how I was hoping my interview would go.

Marianne tilts her head to the side, looking up at me with empathy. "I'm sorry. It's a job, though, and that's good. Get your feet wet in Sweetwater Falls."

"Yeah. I was hoping I could do the only thing I'm good at."

"The only thing?" Marianne asks dubiously. "I think you're pretty good at sizing up a crime scene."

"More like disturbing a crime scene." I double check to make sure no one is within earshot, but it seems like we might be the only two people in the building. "Do you have a minute? Something has been tugging at my brain."

Marianne's eyebrows dance with intrigue. "I have *all* the minutes." She motions around to the empty book-stacks. "Not everyone thinks the library is as amazing as I do."

"Shortsighted, the lot of them," I say with my nose in the air.

She waves for me to join her behind the circular desk in the area for employees only.

My shoulders bounce with importance. "I feel so special, getting to go behind the desk. People are going to think I'm all smart, sitting next to you back here."

Marianne snickers, setting her book to the side. "What's been on your mind?"

I can't believe how easy it is to talk to Marianne, to pour out my musings and expect her to make sense of them before I have.

"The sheriff stopped by the house this morning. He wanted to talk to Winifred about the last time she saw Gerald. Apparently, they'd had a fight and broke up two nights before his body was found. Someone saw it, so the finger has been pointed at Winifred as the most likely suspect."

Marianne's hand over her heart is the cutest thing, and echoes my own woe over my aunt's plight. I take my time explaining the interrogation the sheriff gave my aunt, and then bring up the one point that's got me stuck. "He said there was nothing abnormal about Gerald when he was found, but Marianne, look at the picture."

I feel a little bad that I shove my cell phone under her nose, displaying the photo of the dead body with little warning.

Marianne cringes at the sight. "Oh! Poor Gerald."

"Look at his hands."

Through her grimace, she peers closer, her fingers tugging at her brown braids. "Huh." She squints. "Why would Sheriff Flowers not make a note of his hands? They're orange." She looks at me. "Why are they orange?"

I shake my head. "I don't know."

Marianne shrugs. "Maybe he was painting?"

"Painting what? That's not exactly a shade you would paint your house."

She purses her lips. "I thought we suspected Amos Vandermuth, on account of the two of them having a fight over money before Gerald died."

"Well, I do suspect him, but I'm more worried about the *how* than the *who*, which perhaps is backwards." I blow out a long breath. "I want to meet Amos."

Marianne's neck lengthens as her eyes brighten. "I

know how we can get him in here. He rarely leaves the house unless it involves the Live Forever Club's events, though he complains the entire time."

"How are you going to get him to come to the library, then?"

Marianne's dark eyebrows dance with mischief. "I have more power than most realize. Funny how late fees can sneak up on a person." She taps her computer, which looks to be seriously outdated. With a flourish of triumph, she points to his information and picks up the phone on the desk.

"Such a scoundrel," I tease her with a giddy grin. "What would the upstanding Agnes, Winifred and Karen say about such devious behavior?"

Marianne chews on her lower lip. I can see she is torn, unsure if breaking the rules is worth it, even when murder is on the line. "Maybe I shouldn't..." But it's too late. "Hello, Amos. This is Marianne." She sits straighter when a grousing grumble comes back as the reply. "Yes, well, I thought you should know that you have a copy of..." She casts around, clearly inexperienced with lying. "'Suzy Rides a Bike' was checked out to you, and it's overdue."

I can hear his outrage as clear as if the man were standing before me. "What? I never checked out a book with that title, and I never return anything late. What fee?"

"It's a dime a day, and it says here it's three days late."

"What?" The thunder in Amos' voice makes it sound like he thinks he has been told he owes a thousand dollars. "But I never checked that book out from the library!"

"Oh, really? Well, there's a form you need to fill out to stop the charges while we look into it." She grimaces at what I can tell is a thorough dressing down. "Yes, Amos. I'm here until six, when we close."

She ends the call far paler than she was when she initially picked up the phone.

I let out a loud "Wooh-hoo!" and high-five her for her stellar subterfuge. "That was amazing! Look at you, being all sneaky."

She casts me a wan smile. "Fair warning: if he yells at me in person, I might pee myself."

"I consider myself warned." I glance around at the stacks of books that all look as if they have gone untouched for years. "Amos sure seemed sore about owing thirty cents."

"That's Amos for you. He doesn't believe in tipping, never goes a week without balancing his checkbook, and remembers every person who ever stiffed him. He's got a list."

I snort my disbelief. "You're kidding."

"I've seen it. He carries it in his breast pocket wherever he goes."

I cover my giggle of astonishment. "That is obnoxious."

"That's Amos." Then Marianne slaps her hand over her mouth. "Oh, I'm being mean. I actually do like him. His knack for penny pinching is why I trust him to look over the books for the library's financials whenever I get stuck. Most people can't stand him, but I don't mind it. We all bring something to the table." She pauses, pursing her lips. I can tell she's not satisfied with the amount of praise she's heaped on his name after dressing it down. "He's probably got a reason for being that way. I'm sure I do things that are irritating, too."

"Name one," I challenge her. "Did you forget to thank the birds that braid your hair? Did you sing off-key to the woodland creatures who tuck you in at night?"

"No." We share a chuckle and then switch topics.

She fills me in on the details of the Twinkle Lights Festival, and the various tasks with which she will need my help. Marianne talks with her hands when she is excited, which I find endearing. Anyone who gets this geeked about twinkling lights should have whatever they want, including a second cupcake, which she dives into without hesitation.

I'm starting to like Sweetwater Falls, mostly because of the quirky Live Forever Club, and my new favorite librarian. I see myself staying here longer than the few months I anticipated needing to spend with Aunt Winifred when I thought she needed me to help her get around.

Maybe I could put down roots in this town.

If not for the murder, Sweetwater Falls would be perfect.

SEVEN DOLLARS AND FIFTY CENTS

*M*arianne talks about the Twinkle Lights Festival with such joy that I feel like I've been there in happy dreams or goofy old Christmas specials. Sitting in the empty library together, we are enjoying our time so much that it takes us both by surprise when an old man walks in. His cane sends shuddering clacks through the otherwise silent library.

Marianne stands, as if he is a veteran or someone who has earned her utmost respect. In reality, she is nervous. This must be Amos Vandermuth, whom she lured here with a lie so I could see him and get a feel for how murder-prone this man seems.

"Amos, so glad you could come here. I've got a form for you to fill out to stop the charges of the..."

Amos looks to be in his seventies. He shakes a

knobby finger at her, his face sagging with a scowl. He looks as if he must have been born wearing the sour expression. "I haven't ever checked out a book called Suzy Gets a Whatever. I read the classics and nothing less. I have never turned a book in late, so I want a full report of whoever you find that's stolen my account information. If they are taking out books under my name, that's a problem I won't forgive."

I stand and fix Amos with my cheeriest grin. "Hello. I'm Charlotte, Winifred's grand-niece. I'm new in town."

He eyes my extended hand as if I have picked up dog poop and then tried to shake his palm. "What of it?" His brown cardigan is frayed at the sleeves. I wonder how many decades he has owned it.

"It's nice to meet you." I try my best to be congenial, which is usually a surefire way to coax information out of a person. "I made cupcakes. Do you want one?"

He sniffs the box. "How much?"

"It's free. A gift. A way for me to meet new people."

"Hm." Amos takes his time peering into the box of four cupcakes, and selects the one with the most frosting. "There. Fine."

I push myself into extrovert mode, determined to figure out who killed Gerald so I can clear my aunt's name off the sheriff's list of suspects. "Shame about the man who passed. What was his name?"

Amos grunts in my direction. Though he is mildly stooped, he still seems towering and formidable. "Yeah, well, Gerald wasn't exactly a peach."

"Oh? I don't know much about him. Did you know him well?"

"You could say that. I *was* his best friend." Amos speaks with indignation, as if I should have been handed a brochure upon my arrival to Sweetwater Falls with a list of everyone's lifelong pals.

My hand flutters over my heart. "Oh, I'm sorry to hear that. You must be devastated. Was it sudden?"

Amos scrunches his nose at me, wrinkling his face impossibly more. "He was murdered, so yeah, I'd say it was sudden."

I do my very best acting, widening my eyes and popping open my mouth in shock. "Murdered! I don't believe it! Are you sure?"

Marianne's head keeps turning from me to him and back again as she twists the skin on her knuckles, anxious to even be in the presence of a lie.

"Well, unless he climbed on top of a pile of compose and stabbed himself in the heart, I'd say I'm pretty sure." He sniffs the cupcake but doesn't eat it, depriving me of the joy of watching someone take their first bite.

Marianne picks up the slack when I get distracted. "Gerald was stabbed? How did you hear that?"

Amos pauses, as if he slipped up and revealed too much information. "I, um, I just heard it around town. Small town. People talk."

"Who told you that?" Marianne asks, digging deeper.

Amos waves us off, making it clear he thinks of us as pests. "Oh, never you mind. Gossips, the whole town. Now, where's that form I'm supposed to sign? I'm not paying you for a book I've never even seen." Then he starts grumbling under his breath about who on earth would check out a book with such an insipid title.

"Certainly. Right here." She pulls out a sheet of paper and directs him where to sign.

Amos squints at the page. He takes his glasses out of his pocket and puts them on to examine the print. "Make sure you're not trying to swindle me out of my home. You never know with some people."

"Amos," Marianne scolds him. "You know I would never cheat you."

"Yes, well."

I dial up my new girl anxiety. "Is it really that dangerous in Sweetwater Falls? Should I be worried someone is going to steal from me?"

Amos signs his name and shoves his finger in my face. "My own best friend tried to cheat me out of seven dollars and fifty cents. You never know a person's true colors until they up and swindle you out of your hard-earned money. Keep your wits about you, and you'll land on your feet, young lady. Whatever your name is."

"Charlotte McKay," I remind him. "Winifred's great-niece."

"So you say." Then he waves us off as if we are nothing more than peppy cheerleaders trying to sell him subpar lemonade. "Crazy girls."

When he makes his slow exit, I give Marianne a side-long glance. "Well, he's sure a bucket full of sunshine."

"That's Amos for you."

I cross my arms over my chest, watching him through one of the few translucent windows as he ambles to his golf cart. "He knew how Gerald died, Marianne. Plus, he had a motive. Maybe seven dollars and fifty cents isn't enough for most people to go nuts over, but that might be the threshold for Amos."

Marianne swallows hard, playing with her left braid, fretting while she worries the ends and twirls them around her finger. "Do you really think Amos Vander-muth could have murdered his best friend?"

"I think he could." I watch Amos drive away in his golf cart with my untouched cupcake on his dashboard. "And I think he did."

8

CHARLOTTE THE BRAVE

*M*y feet are killing me. Waiting tables is not my calling. Also, I am fairly certain I'm wearing the wrong shoes for the job.

When I make it home and toe off my two-inch modest heels, my ankles scream at me that tennis shoes would have been a better choice.

Aunt Winifred sings to me from the kitchen. "Welcome home, honey cake."

"I'm glad to be home."

And that's when it hits me that I actually am home. As new as this town is to me, it is slowly becoming mine.

I migrate to the kitchen, inhaling the fragrance of savory meat and what I hope are buttery rolls. "Marianne! I didn't know you would be here tonight. That's a nice surprise. Hi, Agnes."

The women take turns hugging me, and suddenly my feet aren't bothering me at all. I love the warmth they emanate, and the sweet glow they all have from being together and enjoying the evening.

I have friends and family to come home to now.

I really like this.

Winifred takes out a sheet pan of fragrant rolls that look homemade, twisted into knots. "The girls come over every Sunday night. Otherwise we miss out on too much, and it takes forever to catch up. Karen is on her way."

"How is our little jailbird?" I ask as I set down my black waitress apron and sit down at the round table.

Agnes presses a glass of water into my hand and kisses the top of my head before she takes the chair beside me. "She drives by the police station once a day at least and catcalls Sheriff Flowers just to goad him. She's living her best life."

I snicker at the scandal. "I can't believe he just let her go. I expected a chase and a recapture or something."

Winifred waves off my worry. "Oh, the sheriff is always trying to pull a power play with us, but he knows we hold all the cards. Most of us babysat him when he was little, so he knows better than to lock us up for something silly like shoplifting."

I want to inform them that the shop owner has every

right to press charges, and shoplifting is not a victimless crime, but I'm guessing this is the wrong audience for that speech.

"How was work?" Marianne asks, taking the chair on my other side.

"It was long and unfruitful. I was there six hours, and I made twenty-seven dollars in tips."

Winifred shakes her head at my plight. "I'll draw you a bath tonight. Give you some time to think things through."

"Think what through?"

Winifred brushes what smells like garlic butter over the rolls while they are still hot. "The fact that you gave up on your dream too quickly."

My mouth waters at the glorious smells surrounding me.

"I tried, Winifred. They didn't want me for the kitchen. I can't *make* someone hire me."

Though, as I say this, I am guessing if Winifred were in my position, she would find a way to do exactly that. She is fearless and doesn't settle.

Which is pretty much the opposite of me.

I'm glad I came here. Maybe her moxie will rub off on me.

Aunt Winnie slides the rolls into a basket and sets it on the table in the center. "Maybe your dream wasn't big enough. If someone else can control whether or not you get what you want, then you're thinking too small." She holds up her finger, as if it's already solved. "Bath after dinner, young lady. Bubbles and lavender can solve a world of problems."

Agnes raises her glass of sweet tea in a toast. "Amen!"

The front door opens without a doorbell ringing to announce the newcomer. I can't decide if I love the fact that people walk in without permission, or if it is unnerving.

"Something smells like I didn't cook it!" calls a woman's voice from the living room. "Make room for your favorite felon, ladies!"

Agnes and Winifred hoot and holler. They bang their spoons to their glasses to make as much noise as possible to welcome their friend.

"Are they always so lively?" I ask Marianne, who munches on a roll. She waves to Karen when the woman enters the kitchen.

"They're toning it down for your benefit, so you don't get spooked and move back to the big city."

"And miss out on all of this?" I motion to the women high-fiving, hugging, and then dancing as Winifred turns on the radio and starts to sway her hips.

The three of them are ridiculous, and I love it.

Man, I'm old. I am the one who is too tired to stand up, while they have tons of energy and liveliness in their smiles.

Marianne stands when Agnes pulls her to her feet. Though she is shy and giggles nervously, Marianne dances with the women, celebrating the victory of Karen's wild misadventure.

Winifred knows I am tired, but she isn't one to give up on fun simply because it is practical to stay seated. She takes my hand and tugs me gently.

"Fun begets fun," Aunt Winnie tells me. "You haven't been sowing your wild oats as you should."

My rhythm isn't as jaunty as theirs, but I manage to shake my hips and raise my arms in the air with the best of them.

This is the life I never knew I needed. These are the friends and family I have lived for far too long without.

No more. I won't pass up on silliness anymore. I will get my priorities straight for once.

When the song ends, we all find our seats in fits of giggles and compliments about who had the best dance moves. Aunt Winifred is an incredible cook, reminding me just how much I have missed a big family meal. There's no point in cooking a pot roast for one person. But this is a feast meant to bring people together.

Karen spears a carrot that has been cooked with the

roast. It drips beef broth onto her pile of corn. "You wouldn't believe what they feed prisoners. Sweetwater Falls has to up its game. Eggs with no bacon for breakfast. A club sandwich with no chips for lunch. No snacks. I had to guilt the sheriff's son into bringing me my morning tea. And dinner?" Karen shakes her head. "Logan brought me what he was having. I don't understand how bachelors stay alive, eating like that."

"What does Logan Flowers eat for dinner?" Marianne inquires while munching on a portion of potato.

"Microwave meals. Not even ones that smell good. The thing stank like the plastic it came in. I can't even." Karen shakes her head. "A man in his thirties should know how to cook. I gave him a piece of my mind and a few recipes, so hopefully he gets his act together. A growing boy needs nourishment."

I bite back the obvious that if this Logan person is indeed in his thirties, he's not a growing boy any longer.

Dessert comes in the form of cupcakes, which I made last night when I was mulling over Amos' obvious culpability. "Vanilla Swiss meringue on lemon cupcakes," I tell them.

I could take a bite, but I wait for my favorite moment.

One by one, they each take a bite, let out a contented "mm" noise. As predicted, they close their eyes, inhale, then exhale. Just like that, I watch their worries slide away.

Karen licks her fingers while Agnes reaches for a second. "Well, that's just about the best cupcake I've had in my life."

"You said that about the vanilla latte cupcakes that had the butterscotch buttercream frosting," I remind Agnes.

"I was right then, and I'm right now. You have a gift, Charlotte McKay. Winnie was right. You gave up on your dream too quickly. These cupcakes need to have their fair chance to shine."

I swipe my finger through the vanilla Swiss meringue. "I'm not like you all. You see a challenge and you steal the sheriff's keys so you can bust your friend out of jail. I see a challenge and I raise my hand and ask politely. When that doesn't work, I fold."

Marianne rubs my back. "I'm the same way."

"*Were* the same way," Agnes corrects with a knowing look to her. "Now that you know who you want to be, the old you isn't here anymore. It's only Marianne the Wild I see at the table now."

Marianne's chest swells with importance. For a second, I see a flash of the wildness in her eyes that that reflects her new title. In that moment, I see how beautiful a person she truly is. I get a glimpse of the freedom she is capable of if she lets go and steps forward.

Winifred leans over and squeezes my shoulder. "Don't worry. You'll get your sea legs, Charlotte the Brave."

My eyes turn glassy as emotion rises in my throat. I don't have the words to tell her how much I wish that was true. I know I am not brave. I left the big city in part because I never made the leap to take a chance on myself. I went there to open up a cupcake shop, but I ended up doing salad prep at a busy restaurant. They couldn't have cared less what my dreams are.

Maybe I set that precedent by not fighting harder for what I want.

And here I am, wasting my new start and doing the exact same thing. I didn't even truly ask Bill at the diner for what I wanted. Not really.

I didn't stand up for myself.

I motion to Aunt Winnie. "You protested. That's brave. I'm still not sure I'm on board with why, but still, you made signs and a plan to show up for Karen." I hold Karen's tender gaze while Agnes and Winifred high-five each other.

Karen reaches across the table and places her silky hand atop mine. "When was the last time you showed up for yourself?"

The silence that hits the room is the same that echoes through my being.

"I don't know," I finally whisper.

Karen lifts her hand in Winifred's direction. "Winnie, go get me your sign and some paint or a marker or whatever you used."

Winifred trots to the garage.

I try to turn myself invisible so I can escape the shame of a life half-lived without purpose.

When my aunt returns, Karen takes the sign. She reads the angry orange script with a smile that tells me she is truly moved at the lengths her friends went to for her. She tugs on Agnes' sleeve and kisses Winifred's cheek. Then she turns it over and runs her palm over the unblemished white surface.

In perfect old lady calligraphy, Karen dips her fat brush into the paint and swirls the lettering onto the sign.

Marianne holds my hand because she knows, as well do I, that we are about to open our minds to a whole slew of possibilities.

When Karen turns the sign around, it reads "Free Marianne! Free Charlotte!"

My eyes close in appreciation. A wave of love for the new self I hope to become sweeps over me.

When I open my eyes, I look to Marianne to see if she is just as moved.

Her smile is frozen and tight. I can tell she is forcing happiness as she squeezes my hand a little too hard.

"That's lovely. Thank you, Karen," I tell her on behalf of us both.

I can't get a read on Marianne's smile, which looks like fright.

When Winifred comments on the fact that she is never going to stop eating these cupcakes, Marianne's wide eyes fix on my face. Her voice is a little too loud, and her cheeriness terribly forced. "Charlotte, you were going to show me that thing in your room."

"What thing?"

"The skirt I wanted to borrow." She grips my hand as if she is afraid that if she lets go, she will fall into a cavern of lava. "Now."

Marianne tugs me out of my chair while I excuse our quick exit. We dash up the steps and run to the second room on the right, which has been given to me.

I haven't taken the time to decorate it yet, but that hardly matters. The rose wallpaper and matching comforter are homey and cozy, and exhibit more personality than I had in my studio apartment in Chicago.

"Which skirt did you want to borrow? What's the rush?"

Marianne slams the door shut, truly looking every bit of her new title as Marianne the Wild. "What would I need a skirt for?" She shakes her head, her palm still on my door. "Did you see the paint Karen used to make our sign?"

I shrug, not remembering much of note. "Yeah. What of it?"

Marianne's lips press hard together as if she is frustrated having to spell out the obvious to me. "It was orange paint. Your aunt had a tub of orange paint handy to make her sign around the time of Gerald's death."

It takes me a handful of seconds to push out my personal breakthrough as the clues slide themselves into place. "Gerald's hands and arms were orange when we found his body."

I shake my head, unwilling to travel toward the direction the evidence is pointing me.

Marianne is firm that I will face the truth, no matter where it leads. "You know what this means."

"No. No, it can't be." I back up until my thighs hit the edge of my bed. My butt plops atop the mattress. "My aunt isn't a killer."

But as I say it, new logic chases in on the heels of my protest.

Winifred stole keys from the sheriff.

Winifred broke a prisoner out of jail and laughed about it.

Dread curdles my stomach, but the fire in Marianne's eyes confirms that nothing will quell my unease until I get to the bottom of Gerald Forbine's untimely death.

9

BREAKING AND ENTERING

*I*t's a poor idea to go to the sheriff's station after hours. In Sweetwater Falls, Marianne informed me that the police support is an answering machine after seven o'clock. After all, Sweetwater Falls is a safe, small town.

If not for the murder, there would be no need for anyone to lock their door.

"It's not breaking and entering if you have a key," Winifred assures me, though her words make me feel slightly less than certain.

Karen wedges her way to the front of the scrum. The five of us are not exactly inconspicuous, though at least we are using the backdoor, and not the front entrance, as Karen suggested on the way here. "It's the longer one."

Agnes drops the ring, though I can tell it's because we are fumbling around by flashlight and not because she is nervous. "Oh, dear. Butterfingers. Marianne, help an old woman out, will you?"

Marianne and I are tense with apprehension. Winifred, Karen and Agnes might have no qualms about breaking into the police station, but the two of us are terrified of getting caught.

Marianne dips down and scoops up the ring of keys, searching in the thin stream of light for the longest one. "You have to stop stealing the sheriff's things, Winnie. One of these days, he's not going to come peacefully to your house to retrieve them."

Winifred bats away Marianne's concern with a light-hearted scoff. "I didn't steal them this time. I made copies. These are *my* keys, I'll have you know. Made copies for the three founding members of the Live Forever Club. Once you earn your stripes, I'll get a copy made for the both of you, too."

Marianne and I groan in unison. Marianne fiddles with the keys, trying to fit the selected bronze one in the lock. "I hope breaking into the police station earns me lifetime status as a wild woman, because I am never doing this again."

Agnes chortles. "That's what I said my first time."

She leans in, her hand on Marianne's shoulder. "You only live once. Best take it at a run."

Their odd brand of wisdom sits strangely in my stomach, but I don't brush it away as foolishness. My entire life has been spent calculating risk, which usually edges me out of taking the smallest step forward.

I was a salad chef in Chicago with a passion for desserts. I had the opportunity to ask for what I wanted out of life, but I was too afraid of being pushy. Too nervous to step out on a ledge and face the possibility of rejection.

I didn't take my passion at a run. I stood still, and Chicago spat me out.

When the door pops open, Winifred waddles past us. My spine stiffens as a slow beeping warns us that this place has an alarm system designed to tattle on people like us.

Winifred doesn't look worried at all as she approaches the small box on the wall. She even smiles at the angry red light that goes on and off to show us we are not welcome. Her crooked finger punches in a code from memory, and the system goes back to sleep. "Alright, girls," she calls over her shoulder. "Let's do this."

Marianne and I stand still, shocked at the layers of

subterfuge. "Have you done this before?" I ask, my hands on my hips.

Karen makes her way to down the corridor with her flashlight illuminating the path. "Oh, loads of times. But never with my own set of keys. This is far better."

Marianne's hand slides to mine, our fingers locking together. "We are going to be in so much trouble!"

Agnes bats her hand at Marianne's worry. "Only if we get caught, which we never do. Come on. The trick is not to dawdle. We're on the hunt, ladies. Don't forget why we came here."

My insides are churning as I step further into the deceit, Marianne by my side. We follow the Live Forever Club into the main office area, shuffling behind the intake desk. "How are we supposed to find anything?" I wonder aloud as I take in the stacks of forms and files on the front desk.

Karen, our most recent jailbird, pushes us toward the back room. "Information on Gerald's case wouldn't be lying around out here. This is all traffic violations and boring stuff. The open cases are on the sheriff's desk in his office. That's where we're headed." She takes out her key ring and starts jiggling them one by one in the lock. "I swear, I'm going to have a talk with Flowers about having too many keys he doesn't use. What could he possibly need all these for?"

She finally jams the correct one into the knob and opens the door. Marianne and I stand outside the office until Agnes gently pushes us inside.

I should not be in here. Anything that must be done by cover of darkness is most likely a bad idea.

Yet still, I'm doing it. Adrenaline races through my veins. My hands find themselves trembling as I leaf through the pages atop the desks.

"Make sure to keep them in the order he had them!" Marianne frets.

Agnes clucks her tongue, shaking her head at the mess. "You call this order? This is shameful. I'm going to have a talk with him about this."

I can't stop my quiet laughter. Maybe it's part hysteria, but picturing Agnes lecturing the sheriff over the state of his disorganized desk after we broke the law to get here strikes me as comical.

Though I wouldn't put it past her.

Winifred holds up a form. "Here! Is this what we're looking for?"

"We don't know what we're looking for!" I remind them all. "Clues are nebulous. There might not be anything worth finding in here. We might already know all that he does."

Still, I peer over Winifred's shoulder, leaning over Karen's stooped form. A hush falls over all five of us as we scour the pages one by one. I take in some typed information, and some journaled in an untidy scrawl.

Agnes shakes her head. "Poor boy always did have sloppy penmanship. Good thing his son wasn't also cursed with the same penchant for scribbling. Beautiful handwriting, that one."

Karen sniffs at the page. "Start with the day of Gerald's death. That's probably the day before his body was found. I watch crime shows. They always talk about what he did the day he died."

Winifred flips to the next page, locating details gathered thus far. "He was at the restaurant. Says here Gerald's son was interviewed." For my benefit, she adds, "Robert is his name. They work together at the restaurant Gerald owns." Then she catches herself. "*Owned*. I supposed the Spaghetti Scarf belongs to Robert now." She points to the statement taken by Gerald's son.

Marianne reads aloud, still clutching tight to my hand. "It says Robert didn't see his dad the day before Gerald's body was discovered, which is the assumed day of death. According to Robert, Gerald seemed upset about a fight he had with Winifred the previous might, so he went in to the restaurant to work, giving Robert the day off."

Winifred stiffens and then shoves the papers into Karen's hands. "I don't need to hear that."

Karen cups Winifred's shoulder. "No, you don't. You had every right to do what you did."

Marianne and I lock gazes, and I can tell we are thinking the same thing: what did Winifred do?

I voice the question in a less condemning way. "What do you mean, Karen?"

Karen lifts her chin sanctimoniously. "Never you mind. Keep reading that drivel and see if you find anything useful." She hugs my aunt. "It's alright, Winnie."

I need to get to the bottom of this. With every bit of evidence, it's looking more and more like my aunt is the one with blood on her hands.

Marianne keeps reading. "The rest of the testimony says that Robert didn't see his father on the day of his death. Gerald worked at the restaurant and closed with Helen, who may have been the last person to see Gerald alive."

Karen shakes her head, letting us know that more information is not helpful at this point.

"Is there an interview with this Helen person?" I ask, desperate for a new lead.

Marianne and I take our time reading through the sheriff's findings. With every line, I hope to uncover something that leads the chase in the opposite way of Winifred.

"Here," Marianne points out. "It says Helen is on his list of people to interview still."

Marianne's shoulders are just as tight as mine. When we reach the end of the pages, I am grateful we have at least one person to talk to who might have had the opportunity to murder Gerald.

Marianne whispers only to me. "Helen would never hurt a fly."

My hand fixes to Marianne's elbow. My hushed reply is meant only for Marianne while Agnes and Karen lead Winifred away from the sheriff's office. "Well, at this point, she is the only hope I have that Winifred isn't the one who had the murder weapon aimed at Gerald."

I love my aunt, but it is clear to me that there is more to her time with Gerald than she would like the world to see.

10

A THOUGHTFUL GESTURE

*I*t is three days that I try to push my suspicions out of my head. I don't want my cooky aunt to be a murderer. I have long since passed pretending I can look at this case objectively.

Burying myself in work would be ideal, but every hour that I wait tables at the diner feels like a slow leak on my soul. My feet hurt and I have messed up two orders already. As my shift nears its end, I fear the French fry oil has seeped into my skin and hair, permeating me through.

My cell phone buzzes when I am in the kitchen, rolling silverware and wishing for a better job. "Hey, Marianne."

Marianne sounds rushed but still her chipper self. "Can you help me out? I feel bad for Robert Forbine, losing his dad and all. I told them I would pay for them to have a meal at the diner, but I'm stuck at the library shelving books, and there's no end in sight. They'll be there in half an hour."

Her thoughtfulness stops my hands from their mechanical movements. "That's sweet of you. Want me to start a tab, and you can pay it off later this week?"

"That would be amazing. Thank you."

I am struck by the kindness in Sweetwater Falls, grateful that I now live in a place that values generosity and looking out for one's neighbor.

Half an hour later, two customers walk through the door. I don what I hope is a courteous smile. "Robert Forbine?"

The man extends his hand. "That's me. Marianne sent us over."

I shake his hand and then snatch up two menus. "Everything is all set. She called to arrange for your meal to go on her tab. Can I get you folks something to drink?"

The man is in his forties, and sits across from a woman his age who has dark circles under her eyes. Her nose is red and her chestnut hair disheveled. She picks up a napkin to swipe it as her eyes turn glassy.

Yes, this is Robert and his wife. No question. He's the spitting image of Gerald Forbine, complete with mustache. Plus, the woman's tears are indicative of having lost a loved one.

I know I am supposed to get information out of them, but my semi-professional demeanor crumbles in a flood of fretting when the woman sobs quietly into her napkin. "Oh, no. Let me get you a real tissue. How about some hot tea? That always tends to soothe my insides. You poor thing."

She nods gratefully while the unaffected man across from her requests a coffee.

I scramble to get their beverages. I return with a tissue and half a dozen honey packets on the side of her saucer. "You can never have too much honey on a bad day," I explain.

The woman offers me a watery smile through her palpable pain. "Thank you. I like that. I could use some extra sweetness. This whole thing is just..." She waves her hand to indicate that her troubles are too much for her to even talk about them.

Been there, sister.

I note their wedding rings, and ask her husband what he would like to eat, since he seems more capable of speech at the moment.

"Just the number five breakfast. She'll have the... I don't know. What do you want?" I can tell he wants her to stop carrying on as quick as possible. He offers her a raise of the eyebrows, which I can tell he thinks means he is smiling reassuringly at her, but it doesn't even come close. "How about a slice of cherry pie?"

The woman's face pulls. "No. The pie here is terrible. The crust tastes like the box it came in. Just the tea is fine."

Ouch. I haven't tried the pie here to see if that assessment rings true, but I truly hope it doesn't.

She deserves better than that. No way would I feed a crying friend a pie that tastes like cardboard.

I hand the woman a second tissue. "I know just the thing. Leave it to me."

I turn on my heel and put in the man's order. Then I move to my own lunch and pull out a cupcake I brought for myself. The perfect way to travel with a cupcake if you still want the frosting design intact is to drop it into a clear plastic cup, then cover the whole thing with plastic wrap.

I am an expert at few things, but cupcake care is one badge I wear proudly.

I shimmy the dessert out of the cup without denting the frosting in the slightest and put it on a plate.

I don't wait for the husband's order to come; she shouldn't have to be put on hold, waiting for life to bring some cheer to her dismal day.

When I set the plate in front of her, the woman's

shoulders lift at the unexpected offering. "What is this? I've never seen cupcakes at the diner before. Is this new?" She looks around for the owner. "I didn't realize Bill was capable of doing anything new."

"I made it and brought it from home." I give her a little wink. "Thought you could use it more than me today."

The woman rests her hand over her heart. "That's so sweet. I couldn't possibly."

"You can and you will." I tilt my head to the side, doing my best to emanate the compassion I feel for her. "Rough day?"

"Rough week. Rough month. Rough year." She squints her eyes, as if seeing me anew. "You're the new girl in town. Winifred's great-niece, right?"

"That's right."

"Then you probably didn't know him, but my father-in-law passed just recently. Very suddenly and unex-pectedly. It's all a bit overwhelming right now."

I should leave her to her tea and dessert, but I can't help myself. My body folds itself into the booth beside her. "Oh, I'm so sorry. I did hear about that."

And I discovered the body.

And I just so happen to have a picture of the man on my phone as we speak.

I swallow all that and offer a timid, "Just awful," and then wrap an arm around her shoulders.

The woman tears up all over again, but this time manages to keep from sobbing. "Who would kill such a good man? He was a saint, I tell you. An absolute saint. Did everything for his son." She motions to her husband. "We've all worked at the Spaghetti Scarf together since before Robert and I started dating."

Then it most likely wasn't a family member who offed Gerald.

I pat the woman on the back. "Sounds like you three were quite close."

She nods into my shoulder. "We were. He was always there for us. Last month, he even came over to unclog the sink when we couldn't get the disposal working. Always made time for us."

Robert fiddles with the napkins in the holder, keeping his eyes on the stack. "Well, let's be honest, Roberta. He had less time for us lately. He had his own life, his own things going on. Let's not rewrite history just because he's dead."

I bite my tongue to keep from scolding the man. I mean, what a thing to say. Even if it's true, this clearly isn't the time.

Still, I guess if anyone gets to set the tone for how to grieve for Gerald, it should be the man's own son.

Also, it just dawns on me that they are a married couple name Robert and Roberta. My inner goofball giggles at the cuteness, but the adult woman in me maintains a compassionate demeanor.

I give Roberta another squeeze before releasing her. "Tea. Tea and a cupcake. That's what the doctor ordered. I'll keep bringing you tissues as often as you need."

"Bless you..." Roberta pauses and squints at my nametag. "Charlotte. Bless you, Charlotte."

I excuse myself and tend to my other tables, who have gone woefully ignored.

At the diner, the waitress is also the person who busses tables and rolls silverware, which I am behind on. I set to work, wishing Sweetwater Falls had just one bakery for me to apply to. I could be spending my days baking cupcakes, instead of scrubbing the bacon grease off of booths because I cannot in good conscience let another customer stick to the vinyl.

Gross.

I bring out Robert's food and more tissues for Roberta when the order comes up. I expect her to have picked at the cupcake. I mean, she didn't exactly say she was craving dessert. I just wanted to bring her something sweet as more an offering of human decency, rather than because sugar is the thing she desired. No matter how delicious my cupcakes are, kindness is always what people are hungry for, I have learned.

When I set Robert's food down in front of him, I notice the cupcake has been reduced to a few crumbs. Roberta is sticking them to her finger so she can finish up those, as well.

I missed the glory of her first bite, which is my favorite part to watch, but this is just as satisfying a sight.

Roberta gapes up at me, her tears dried on her cheeks in streaks. "Young lady, did you say you made this?"

"I did." I beam at her, unable to hold back my pride. "It's a vanilla latte cake with a butterscotch buttercream frosting."

I probably make this a little too often, but I love them.

Be brave. Be brave. Winifred's prayer for me chimes in my ears.

Instead of clamming up, I lift my chin and bunch my toes in my shoes, bolstering myself as much as I am able. It takes all my gusto, but I manage to speak boldly what I want to the universe. "I was actually hoping Sweetwater Falls had a bakery in the city where I could sell my cupcakes, but it's looking like cardboard cherry pie is all I've found."

Roberta shakes her head. "Oh, no. Have you worked in a kitchen before?"

"Yes. In Chicago."

I don't mention that my kitchen prowess was salad prep, which consisted of copious chopping and zero baking.

She wiggles her finger between herself and her husband. "Robert and I are now the sole owners of the Spaghetti Scarf. It's the Italian place over on Apple Blossom Street. Maybe this weekend, you could stop by and bring over a few more flavors for me to sample. I wouldn't be opposed to seeing if we could fit your items on our menu."

I balk at the good fortune. "Are you serious? I would love that."

Marianne sent the Forbines over to see if I could gather information from them; I don't think she was counting on them offering me an audition for the job of my dreams.

Robert looks reluctant, but nods once. "Sure. Now that Dad is gone, we can actually give the menu an update. He never changed a thing. Even the welcome mat is the same one it's been for the past decade." He motions to his wife. "Anything that can perk up Roberta deserves a chance to shine." He glances up at me and extends his hand. When I shake his firm grip, praying my palm isn't clammy, he fixes me with an expression that's all business. "I'm in this weekend during the day. Bring your samples and ask for me. I don't mind taking a chance on the new kid, so long as every cupcake you have can make my wife smile like that."

Roberta does have a softness to the curve of her lips. As gruff as Robert came off earlier, I do like it when a man goes the extra mile for his wife's smile.

"Thank you so much. You won't be disappointed. I'll see you Saturday with the best desserts you've ever tasted."

I walk away from the table feeling taller than I did this morning when I got dressed. My spirits are lifted sky high because I did it.

I was brave.

11

CARDAMOM CLUMSINESS

*a*fter I clock out, I don't go straight home. I get directions from Winifred over the phone to the nearest (and only) grocery store. I zip to the general store in Sweetwater Falls, hoping it has all I need on its shelves. When I pull into the place, the sign overtop reads "Colonel's General Store".

Colonel General.

I get a little giggle out of that. I like cutesy names for things.

From the outside, the place looks like a long, one-story log cabin. On the inside, the shelves are made of wood. The place carries everything from tackle for fishing to nylons to actual food for humans.

I grab a cart and hope the stench of burger grease

isn't stuck to my skin as I pass an endcap with perfect lines of canned dog food.

In fact, as I move through the aisles, I find that everything in the store is in perfect perpendicular lines, with the labels facing the consumer.

I like it here.

When I pass the tea and coffee aisle, I throw a box of turmeric tea into my cart, knowing turmeric helps with joint pain and inflammation. If that is what is causing Aunt Winifred's limp, hopefully the tea will soothe her aches without bringing undue attention to them.

Three sacks of flour, two sacks of granulated sugar, brown sugar, powdered sugar, eggs, milk, and all the standards for my cupcakes find their way into my buggy. Then I search for the more obscure ingredients that are far easier to find in a big city.

When I don't find dried hibiscus flowers, because of course I don't, I close my eyes and take a deep breath. I have to remind myself that my best creations come to me when I need to replace my standards with new ingredients. The necessity of stretching myself in the kitchen isn't always pleasant, but it makes me come alive.

I guess I could use a bit more life in my world. If I am going to keep up with Winifred, I can't afford to let my imagination go stagnant.

I veer toward the spices, which is a tried and true standard for reinventing the familiar. Cinnamon, cloves, allspice and the like are easy ways to brighten a predictable piece.

But I don't need this to be easy.

I need to be brave.

I know what easy gets a girl. The easy way produces cherry pies that taste like cardboard. There is no love in that path.

I may not know all the secrets of life, but I know love when it pounds in my chest. I know how to bake a dessert that can make a grown man cry.

I will not take the easy route. There is no reward in playing it safe.

My vanilla cupcake is to die for, but I know that if I open my mind, my kitchen has a new song it is waiting to sing. I only need to let the ingredients have a voice.

Another breath in and out, and my eyes land on the perfect ingredient. I know this is the path before I have even plotted out the recipe.

Cardamom, black pepper and allspice find their way into my cart. I don't chuck them in the basket, but set them in with love and affection, appreciating them for the song they are about to sing for me. I run my fingers over the labels, smiling softly because together we are about to crack open a whole new world of flavor for this small town.

"I've never seen anyone cradle spices before," comes a male voice to my left.

I startle, suddenly remembering that I am not in private, but in the middle of a general store, acting like a weirdo. I shrink as I turn toward the other customer.

I mean to say... I'm not sure what exactly. Hopefully I was aiming for something clever. But when the sight of the man with honey-colored neatly cut hair, broad shoulders and a trim waist fills my vision, all words desert me.

When I offer nothing by way of conversation, he peers into my buggy. "Cardamom? I daresay you might be the first person to buy that particular spice in Sweetwater Falls. Might want to check the date." He glances around. "Though, the Colonel doesn't tolerate imperfections, so you're probably safe there."

His grin is just as charming as his easy demeanor. Doggone it, he has dimples screwed into both cheeks, making his angular jaw and high cheekbones impossibly more impressive.

And I am standing in front of him—the prettiest man I have seen in I'm not sure how long—mute and stupid.

All traces of my earlier bravery desert me in a stuttering breath. He is expecting some sort of reply, but all I manage is an incoherent "mmhmph."

I am not sure what I was going for there, but he doesn't appear put off by my ineptitude.

"You're the new girl, right? Winifred's niece?" He dips his head in my direction. "Sorry. Not much new happens in Sweetwater Falls. You've become everyone's favorite topic."

I cannot imagine a more boring topic. "Really?"

There. That was a word. Well done.

I reach for anything to take my eyes off of him, focusing on a jar on the shelf and turning over the label. I'm sure he can tell I was ogling.

I never ogle. I smile courteously. I make small talk. I go on three dates. I politely decline the fourth. I stop returning phone calls.

He nods, flashing me a perfect smile without a hint of mirth. "The girl who found Gerald."

I grimace. Of course that's why I'm known around town.

The t-shirt model seems to understand the conversational misstep, and backpedals quickly. "Sorry. I shouldn't have brought that up before even introducing myself. You probably don't want to think about dead bodies at the grocery store." He shakes his head at himself, no doubt blaming my muteness on himself.

Poor guy doesn't realize that his degree of handsomeness will seal my lips no matter how gregarious he might be.

Please talk to anyone else, I want to beg him. I am no good at connecting with people who are lightyears more attractive than normal humans.

He extends his hand. "I'm Logan."

"I'm... Oh, no!" The thing I've pulled off the shelf at random slips from my hand, smashing between us in a splash of pickle brine and eggs. "I'm sorry!"

Pickled eggs? In the baking aisle? Why?

And why did I grab the jar of it? Why did I have to drop it?

The stench of pickled eggs fills the aisle and no doubt the entire store within seconds.

He holds up his hands. "Careful, there's broken glass. Are you okay?"

Don't also be a nice person. There's only so much a girl can take!

I can't manage a full sentence, so I work out a bleat of "M-fine." I glance around for a store clerk, and just as I turn, one comes trotting toward us.

"The Colonel isn't going to like this," the woman

grumbles. While I should think she would scurry off to gather up a mop, she stills. Her head tilts to the side and shifts her red frizzy hair to her shoulder. "Oh, you're the new girl. The one who found Gerald."

I need to get a better reputation.

I twist my fingers, my nerves at their breaking point. "I'm so sorry. I had a clumsy moment. I'll pay for the jar I broke."

As I turn to more fully face the woman I have wronged, my heel slips on the slick brine, and I lose my balance. My arms flail like the klutz I always am at the exact wrong moment. My hips wobble as if I am on my way to losing a hula hoop contest.

My arms flail out to grab onto anything that might stop this *Three Stooges* moment from unfolding, but I miss the shelf completely. My hand slams down on my cart, pushing the whole thing away from me and exacerbating my descent toward the mess that much more horribly.

Strong arms reach out, wrapping around my body quicker than I can make sense of their direction. One hand fixes under my elbow while the other coils around my midsection, stopping my fall midway.

A gust of relief comes out of me. But the moment I realize the hands that steadied me belong to the beautiful Logan, I wish the brine and broken glass would have taken me instead. Horror twists my features. I shouldn't be this near someone so intimidatingly pretty. He definitely should not be holding me.

"Easy, Charlotte," he tells me in a gentle yet firm manner. The steadiness of his of voice makes me think no one has ever had cause to be cross with this man.

He has bright green eyes. When I come face-to-face with him as he rights me, that is the only thing that registers. They are the color of grass after it has just rained—deep and beautiful and filled with kindness that chases away all the shadows.

I am not used to being this close to someone so wholly handsome. My entire body is blushing, heated by the unassuming touch.

Logan steers me away from the mess, keeping his hand on my elbow while he drags my buggy down the aisle. "You alright? No injuries?"

I need to get away from him before I have another clumsy moment and pull the shelf down on our heads.

"Only death by embarrassment," I admit. I am cloaked in stupidity, wearing it for the world to see.

If it wasn't clear that Logan is out of my league before, that little stunt sure seals it.

He laughs at my turn of phrase. The sound of his

velvety timbre teases me, while my smarter self wants to run for the door before I have another klutzy catastrophe. "Well, we wouldn't want that."

Logan is polite to me, which is the worst. I feel like I'm his elderly aunt or something as he steers me into the next aisle. We pass the store clerk with the mop in tow, who no doubt curses the day I was born.

If my face could turn a deeper shade of red, I am fairly certain we would be veering into purple hues. I want to abandon my cart and run out of the store altogether, but as I actually do need the ingredients in my buggy, that is not an option.

"Checkout. Thanks-bye," I manage as I pull myself from the handsomest man in Sweetwater Falls, and quite possibly, the world.

I don't look up as I thrust my things onto the checkout conveyor belt, but get through the task as quick as possible. I can feel Logan watching me surreptitiously as he examines a pouch of coffee on an endcap near the register.

I drop three things, entirely because he is watching. His gaze makes me clumsy.

I finally make it out of the store and shove all my groceries into my car. I peel out of the parking lot with no finesse, still blushing and reeking of chagrin.

As I replay the horror over and over in my mind, I am certain that there is no coming back from that horrid introduction.

It's just as well; I have no business being near someone that pretty.

FISHING WITH FRIENDS

*W*hen I get home from the debacle at the grocery store, the garage is open. It's always shut when I come home, but today, Winifred is fishing around in the space, trying to grab something off a shelf. She stands on her tiptoes, reaching high.

When she spots my car, she finally gives up, flagging me down.

Instead of my usual spot, I park on the left side of the garage, so as not to crowd my aunt.

She greets me with a hug, and for a second, the urge to spill my embarrassment all over her in a gust occurs to me. "Hi, honey cake. How was work?"

"My day was amazing, and then it was a disaster. What are you trying to reach?"

"The box up there. It's got my fishing gear. I'm going

to the creek with Karen and Agnes. I can't for the life of me think of how I got my tackle box up there to begin with."

"I'll grab it." It's barely any effort to take the worn, olive-colored hard case down, being that I am taller than most. "There you go."

Winifred feigns a swoon. "My hero! I can't think back to what I did before you came along. Maybe I was taller back then." She chortles to herself, examining the box. Her smile turns wistful, twisting from cheerful to precious, tinged with a note of melancholy as her head tilts to the side. "Gerald was supposed to take me fishing today. The girls didn't miss a beat. They're taking me fishing so we can talk about it all while pretending we care about something as boring as fishing."

My body stills as I take in her plans. I've never had friends like that. I've always wanted women who knew me enough to predict my ups and downs, who knew what I needed and planned their weekends around my grief.

My shoulders lower. "I think that's lovely. What a sweet way to pay honor to his memory."

She looks down at the tackle box, holding it at both ends like she is presenting it to herself. She blinks a few times. "Grief is hard. Friends help."

It's a simple truth, but it's so profound that it conks me over the head with its veracity.

My hand finds its way to rest atop hers. "I'm glad I came here. I want to help you. Really help. I mean, clearly you don't need looking after. But what do you need? How can I be a good friend?"

A small smile finds her weathered lips. "Just keep asking that. Eventually, I'll stop being so stubborn and I'll have an answer. Until then, keep the cupcakes coming."

"I can do exactly that."

A golf cart pulls up in the driveway with Karen at the wheel. "Come on, Winifred. If we don't get to the creek before nightfall, we won't get the good fish."

I snigger in her direction, blowing Agnes a kiss. "Is that the way it works?"

Karen shrugs. "We have no idea how it works. I borrowed fishing poles. Winnie's got the tackle box. Agnes brought the bait. I feel like that should hook us the good fish."

Agnes holds up a picnic basket. "Worms, shrimp, strawberries and grapes. I thought we could experiment to see which bait the fish prefer."

I love these three; I can't help it. "My money's on the grapes."

Agnes winks at me as Winifred gets into the back of the golf cart, shifting aside the poles.

Aunt Winnie claps twice. "Let's go, ladies. I was supposed to be hearing sweet nothings and blushing right about now."

Karen raises her hand. "I can do the sweet nothings! Winifred, you're a vision. An absolute dream girl."

Agnes hoots her amusement as Karen backs down the driveway. "That's right. Winnie, you're the light of my life. The first fish I catch I'll name after you."

Winifred swoons as Karen turns onto the road. "So romantic!"

I laugh through my nose, waving at the three until they drive out of sight. They are the best.

I want that. Life would be glorious if I had a friend with whom I could share the good and the bad.

It's an effort to push myself to step out on the edge of my daring, but I take out my phone as I head back to the garage and make the call anyway. Marianne and I have hung out several times. I don't know why calling someone on the phone makes my insides tighten up. But the fact that I hesitate means bravery is needed.

And I am Charlotte the Brave.

My chest puffs as the call connects. "Hey, Charlotte. I was just thinking about you."

My shoulders relax. "What a coincidence. The ladies

just left to go fishing, and I got a bit lonely for a girl-friend. How's your day going?"

I start sliding my groceries out of the back of my car.

"Slow. Sweetwater Falls doesn't read enough. It gives me too much time to think about who could possibly have murdered Gerald. Feel like company tonight? I know I'm not going to sleep until we've talked this through. And I mean *all* the way through."

I cradle the phone between my cheek and my shoulder. "You have excellent timing. I'm about to be up all night baking. Come on by when your shift is over. We can eat frosting while we put our detective hats on."

I can hear Marianne's smile in her reply. "Perfect. See you in an hour."

Ending the call apparently requires too much coordination from me. In an effort to keep my device from smashing on the concrete floor of the garage, I drop the sack of flour and a bag of groceries from my grip.

At least a jar filled with pickling liquid didn't smash this time.

I cringe, still mortified at the memory of having made such a fool of myself in front of Logan.

I pocket my phone, scolding myself for being such a klutz.

When I pile the things back into the grocery bag, it's then that I realize something my eyes have been blocking out. On the floor of the garage is splattered a three-foot-long smear of orange paint.

My stomach drops when I realize this is the same shade as the color I saw on Gerald's hands and arms.

It was a coincidence when Marianne pointed out the orange paint before. I could write that off because Winnie had seen Gerald two nights before he was discovered dead. It's possible she was making her sign near him and he happened upon her paint.

Perhaps they had been painting Karen's freedom signs, and he'd gotten some paint on his hands. That doesn't make Winifred the one who killed him.

But studying the splatter pattern, this doesn't look like a peaceful breakup. I can imagine all sorts of angry words and emphatic hand gestures that might accompany a mess this large.

If I had to guess, this fumbling streak of orange tells me the two of them didn't have an amicable breakup, but one that involved throwing paint and who knows what else.

I try to retrace Winifred's steps in my mind's eye. Maybe she broke up with him and he didn't take it well. Perhaps he grew angry and wanted answers. Maybe he thought she was cheating on him, or something less savory than "this just isn't working out."

My gaze touches on the corner where there is a

worktable. No doubt this is where they were decorating their signs. Maybe he grew aggressive, and she picked up a tub of paint to throw at him. Then maybe his anger picked up and she had to defend herself with something heavier.

Like any number of the gardening tools she has hanging along the wall.

The whole scene makes so much sense, but I still don't want to believe it. My mind tells me I am right in following this logic, but my gut screams that Winifred is a good person who would never murder a person.

At least, that's what I hope.

13

MERINGUE AND MURDER THEORY

*B*aking cupcakes is not a task that can be rushed. It is comforting to know that if I mix eggs, sugar, butter and vanilla into flour, baking soda, and salt, it will always turn into cupcakes.

Sometimes the whole world needs more sugar; other times, it's just me who can't go another day without creating something that sweetens my life.

Tonight, on my fourth batch of cupcakes, Marianne and I have gone over the details of Gerald's murder too many times to count, but we are still nowhere solid.

Marianne scrubs my mixing bowl for the seventh time tonight. "So you're positive it both *has* to be Winifred, and also that it *can't* be her."

"Yes."

She narrows one eye at me to give me a glimpse of her wry humor. "Nothing confusing about that."

"And you're still positive it's Amos Vandermuth?"

Marianne nods. "I can't shake it. He cares about money an unhealthy amount. I mean, you saw how livid he was about possibly having to pay a few dimes in late fees." Her shoulders slump. "But on the other hand, I like Amos. He helps me with the books for the library on occasion. It feels just as wrong to point the finger at him."

"True. But being a miser doesn't make you a murder."

"Neither does being clumsy with orange paint," she points out. "I just don't believe Winifred would murder a man."

"Me neither," I admit. "But I can't discount the evidence just because I love her, or because she's family." My eyes close. "She's been limping."

"She's not exactly a teenager."

"Sure, but is she limping because of arthritis, or because she was just in a physical altercation that ended with her murdering a man?"

We both go silent as the question settles in the air.

I chew on my lower lip, my heart aching that I'm entertaining such thoughts. Though, as much as I'd like to dismiss them, I can't brush them aside.

"Change the subject, I beg of you," I insist as my angst climbs too high for my tolerance.

Marianne snorts. "I can't believe they're out fishing in the evening. They're too funny."

My mouth firms as I whip the eggs for the Italian meringue by hand. "That *is* weird. I didn't think about that before. I've never heard of night fishing."

Marianne stills, and then slowly turns her head toward me. "Not that I believe Winifred did it, but if I was going to dump a murder weapon or some sort of evidence, I would do it at the creek under cover of night. Preferably with an alibi, like fishing with friends."

The fact that Marianne comes to this conclusion has me reeling. My gut doesn't want it to make this much sense, which is no doubt why I didn't get there sooner.

Then, as if Marianne doesn't want to be caught saying anything that might throw me further down that trail, she corrects hard with a cheery, "But that's not what they're doing. They're fishing. They're just really, really bad at it. I still think Amos did it. Though, that doesn't make me feel any better." She sets the mixing bowl in the drainer and picks up a spatula, running the dishrag over it. "Then again, Amos didn't bury evidence, claiming there was nothing odd about Gerald's body when his hands and arms were orange."

I touch my nose and then point to her. "Yes. We can't

discount Sheriff Flowers. That's evidence, right there." My whisk stills in the bowl. "Evidence he could have planted on Winifred. He could have taken the orange paint from her garage and slathered it on Gerald's hands after killing him to point his colleagues in the wrong direction."

Marianne's mouth pulls to the side. "Then why is he burying the evidence of that? Why not make it a top priority to find where the orange came from?"

I consider this, whipping up the meringue with less vigor than the egg whites require. "Maybe he left evidence of himself being there at the crime scene, so the diversion would actually lead them straight to him."

This seems to satisfy Marianne. As she finishes the last of the dishes, she sighs heavily. "I hate this whole thing. I thought last year would be the worst ever, but this one has a murder in it, so I guess my life isn't getting better every year, like I was hoping."

I don't pry, though I do want to know what made last year Marianne's worst year ever.

I taste the meringue, unimpressed with the normal flavor. It's fine, which isn't what I was going for. Not when I will be using these cupcakes to audition for a spot doing what I love at a restaurant.

No shortcuts. Only the best.

It's an extra step, but I scoop some white sugar into

the food processor, along with the guts of a vanilla bean and a handful of shelled cardamom. Pulsing the motor, I blend it all until the sugar is refined but not powdered, and the flavors are well mixed.

Marianne leans in when I take off the lid. She inhales deeply, her eyes rolling back. "Oh my goodness. That smells incredible. Please tell me I get to sample whatever it is you're putting that on."

"Of course. You're my taste tester. But you have to be mean. You can't be polite. I don't want to bring in cupcakes that taste boring."

Marianne salutes me. "I'll be ruthless, Cupcake Commander."

I place a scoop of the new sugar into a pan and melt it down to make a glaze.

Though Marianne and I are still new to each other, at the risk of being nosey, I go out on a limb and poke at her previous words. "You mentioned last year was rough. What happened?"

Marianne plops down in a chair at the table, drying her hands on a rag. "You don't want to know."

I touch my bare toe to hers. "Try me."

She leans her elbows on the table and props her chin up on her fists. "It's fodder for town gossip. Embarrassing, really. We were engaged and he cheated. Jeremy moved out of Sweetwater Falls to go chase his dreams of being a country singer, and he took the girl he was cheating on me with along for the ride."

My upper lip curls on principle. "Yuck. He sounds terrible. I can't believe he did that to you."

Marianne's shoulders slump. "Yeah, well, it was going on a lot longer than I realized. The cheating," she clarifies. "Apparently everyone knew except for me. I was naïve. We were junior high sweethearts. Dated all through high school and beyond. He proposed four years ago, but whenever we had conversations about setting the date, he dodged them." She sits back and points to herself. "See? Naïve."

"I don't think trusting the man you know best makes you naïve. I think it makes you amazing, and makes him a jerk."

Marianne casts me a wan smile. "Thanks. Jeremy the jerk. I like it." She waves off my concern. "It's all fine. Every now and then he sends me a postcard. I'm over it."

I gape at her. "Why is he sending you postcards? He cheated on you and broke your heart!"

Marianne dips her finger into one of Winifred's plastic bowls, where I have been storing my batches of frosting. She sucks on the digit, breathing in and out through her nose before she pops her finger back out. "He's out living his life, and I'm here, doing nothing with mine. I'm boring. I'm the same person I've always been, and there's no end in sight."

I purse my lips, finding several things wrong with her assessment. "First off, you're a lot of fun. Not many have the stomach to sit around on a Thursday night and talk about murders. And people who read aren't boring. They are going on adventures every day. You're an adventurer at heart; you just haven't gotten off the bench in a while."

"Understatement, but thanks."

I set down the meringue and start shoving things into the fridge for safekeeping. "We are not boring," I rule, determined now more than ever to prove how true that is. "We are going to do something fun. Do you keep Jeremy's postcards?"

I know the answer before she says it.

"Yes."

"Good. We are going to your place to grab them, and then we're going to do something fun and unpredictable, because that is the wild sort of woman you are."

She blinks at me, looking lost and forlorn. "I am?"

I nod, tugging her out of her seat and shoving her toward the door. "Get your shoes on."

"What about the cupcakes? You need to finish them, Charlotte."

"I will later. This is more important." I fix her with a smile while mischief dances in my eyes. "Marianne the Wild has her destiny to fulfill."

I put in a call to Winifred, telling her to grab the girls, ditch the fish and meet up with us.

If I have to be brave, then Marianne is going to be wild—even if it is only for one night.

14

FIRELIGHT BRAVERY

*K*aren's wiry smile is a thing of beauty. She truly does look like a jailbird set free, though I wonder if that has always been her way. Her smile lines are engrained in her face, framing her brown eyes and pink-painted lips. "Anything that involves fire is a yes in my book."

Marianne clutches a shoebox to her chest, clearly torn between frightened and excited, which appear to be two sides of the same coin. "I don't know about this."

Agnes' arm hasn't left Marianne since I announced the plans for the night. It has remained curved around Marianne's back, with her other hand occasionally rubbing up and down Marianne's bicep. Whatever move Marianne makes, her makeshift big sister is going to go there with her.

I love it.

Winifred sets two more split logs down in the fire pit, and then crumples up some newspaper to shove underneath.

She owns an axe. I take notes in my head, filing that away as a possible murder weapon.

But Winifred isn't a killer. She can't be. I refuse to believe that this woman I love has evil lurking in her bones.

My aunt's hands are deft at striking the match and lighting the paper. Before long, the fire is crackling and marshmallows are being roasted, because that is what you do when you are having a girl night.

Winifred goes into the house while Karen pokes at the fire with a long stick. "I love a good campfire. This one looks like it could use some more kindling, though. What do you say, Marianne?"

Poor Marianne looks on the verge of either laughing hysterically or vomiting. "Are we sure this is the thing to do?" She clutches the box to her chest. "I mean, what if Jeremy and I get back together someday? I might want the things Jeremy gave me."

I stand near the fire, warming my hands and keeping my gaze on the orange and yellow licking the wood. "You kept a few things that were important to you. Enough for you to look back decades from now and remember the good times. But the rest isn't worth holding tight to." I turn my chin and level my focus on her. "*He* isn't worth holding tight to."

Karen raises her fist. "Hold tight to the good times, burn the bad. Only look back in the rearview mirror when the cops are chasing you." She sits back in the lawn chair, cozying into position. She throws Marianne a wink. "Maybe not even then."

Agnes inches closer to the fire, bringing Marianne along with her. "You only live once, but if you keep clinging to that box, you'll live with a ghost of someone who deserves to be forgotten. Let some other poor soul cling to a box of him. You have too much purpose and promise for that."

Maybe we are goading Marianne on too much. This has to be *her* step forward, not one we do for her. All we can do is keep the fire going and be patient.

Winifred ambles out with a tea tray. It's laden with a steaming teapot of the turmeric tea I bought her, five delicate cups and five of my vanilla cardamom cupcakes. "Here we go, girls. Can't have roasted marshmallows without tea. It's uncivilized." Her limp is slightly better than it was last week, but it is still noticeable. Poor thing.

We all take our cups, staring into the flames as we sip slowly. The fire is hypnotizing, lulling us into a state of peace I didn't realize I had been seeking. When

Winifred catches my eye, she winks at me, trading her secret smile for mine.

Though I am still almost certain she killed Gerald, I cannot bring myself to dig deeper. If she is a murderer, so be it. She is still my family, and for now, that is enough to quiet any unsettled parts of my spirit.

The rest will figure itself out.

For now, there is only tea. Only campfire. Only marshmallows. Only cupcakes.

Only Marianne's clear angst.

The quiet settles in on us, calming my nerves and washing away any hint of unease. I love how clear the night sky is in Sweetwater Falls. There isn't as much light pollution, so the stars pop ever more visibly. "This isn't a moment you can get in the city."

Agnes keeps her arm affixed to Marianne's shoulder, her side tucked tight to her little sister's. "It's a moment we wouldn't have had tonight at all, if our city girl hadn't suggested it. Life is what you make of it. I think that tonight, we are going to make a new memory." She kisses Marianne's temple. "A new future."

Another blanket of silence falls over us, filled in only by the crackling of the fire and the shifting of the wood as it burns.

I truly have missed out on this portion of living. I've filled my life with second-guessing and shutting up, when I could have been warming the parts of me that threaten to ice over for good.

A sound so faint, I nearly miss it at first, wafts through the evening air. The sun is setting, giving the moon full use of the sky. I can hear a lovely hum, a melody that takes shape and draws me in.

Karen is singing. She has a voice that strikes me as both precious and powerful, coaxing the night to let us be part of its magic. The tune gives birth to a song that fills my soul in ways I didn't realize I needed.

The refrain comes three times between verses stacked with oaths of loyalty and love.

"MINE, MY DEAR.
 Mine, your love.
 Mine, my sweet.
 Thine, my all."

MY HEART CAN BARELY TAKE THE EMOTION THAT CRESTS every time Karen sings the chorus. I'm not sure if it's the words, her angelic voice, the campfire, or the combination of all three, but I find contentment easier than I am usually able. The burnt smell of the wood permeates my hair and clothing, reminding me that not everything has to be a step forward. Sometimes it is necessary for me to just be.

Be in the moment.

Be with friends.

Be myself, however strange that person might be.

Winifred steps up to the campfire ring with a card in her hand. "I was going to give this to Gerald. I saw it at the grocery store and thought it was funny. Thought it would make him smile. I didn't even have an occasion picked out. It was a 'just because' sort of thing." She bows her head, stilling before the fire as she hugs the greeting card. When my aunt lifts her head again, she tosses the card into the fire. "Rest well, Gerald."

I don't even realize my eyes are damp until my breathing hitches. I didn't know the man, but in this short time I have lived in Sweetwater Falls, I feel as if I understand a side of my aunt I never knew before. It's inspiring to watch her love so openly and live without regret.

Even now, she burns the token of her affection for the man, knowing it will not bring him back.

When Winifred steps away from the fire, I help her to sit in her lawn chair. I don't comment on the tremble in her hands when I press her teacup between her palms. With gentle fingers, I wipe away the tear that has fallen onto the apple of her cheek.

With her free hand, Winifred grips my fingers. "Don't say no to the unknown. Don't let worry get the best of you, little sister."

The nugget of truth blasts me with its potency. All the time, I let worry get the best of me.

I squeeze her hand, willing her words to guide me. "I won't."

My insides glow with warmth. Genetics have made me her great-niece, but love and choice have made me her little sister. I love it.

I love her.

When movement catches my eye, I turn and see Marianne approaching the fire. "Jeremy was everything to me," Marianne admits. "Maybe I let my world become too small because of it. I didn't see what was obvious to everyone in town—that he was a cheater."

Agnes migrates to her side. "What is obvious to us is that you are better than him. Take that with you. Nothing else."

Marianne nods once and then opens the shoebox. A teddy bear topples into the fire, sending smoke up as the flames devour the poor animal. Next comes a series of letters, all eager to become kindling. "I kept only the best parts of him in a separate box. These are all the love notes he wrote to me while he was cheating."

I am so proud of Marianne. Watching her stand up

for herself is admirable. Witnessing the wild flash of daring in her eyes as the last of the items sizzle and burn in the fire pit is a thing of beauty.

As I look around at the women who are only lit by the fire, the stars and their own internal force, I am grateful I came to Sweetwater Falls. I want to be one of these incredible women.

And somehow, I finally am.

Just like them, I am wild.

And just like them, I am finally brave.

15

CUPCAKE NEGOTIATIONS

I was bold last night, stepping a foot forward into my instinct. Instead of the vanilla cupcakes I know will sell just fine, I glazed each cake with the cardamom vanilla glaze before topping them with a vanilla meringue. The combination made me swoon, but at the end of the day, it doesn't matter what I love; it matters what Robert can sell.

Standing in the parking lot of the Spaghetti Scarf and staring at the sign, I wonder if this is my chance, or if I will always be searching for a place where my dream can to come to light.

Clutching the box of cupcakes in my hands, I don't recall an ounce of the bravery that led me to this moment. I remember very little of the raised chin I felt in the glow of the firepit. As I stand outside of my car, it occurs to me that I very easily can turn right back around and go home. No harm, no foul.

No rejection.

No risk.

Anxiety ramps up, reminding me that I am no good at this. I am a rule-follower. I take direction well. I harmonize in the background, knowing a solo is well out of my comfort zone.

I can't do this.

I turn back around and slide my cupcakes in the passenger's seat. This is too big a push. I want this too badly. If it doesn't happen—if Robert rejects my cupcakes—I will be devastated. At least this way, if I go home now, I will only be mildly discontent, which is a far cry from devastation.

As if she can feel me chickening out, my phone buzzes in my pocket with Winifred's name on the screen. "Hey, big sis. Do you need me to pick anything up from the store for you?" I figure a quick subject jump will help me be able to hide from her disappointment, and my own.

"What do you think you're doing?"

My brows push together. "Coming home. Why?"

"Did you show your cupcakes to Robert?"

The sigh is probably all I need to give her, but she

deserves actual words, I suppose. "It's a bad idea. I made the wrong flavors. He's not going to like these."

"Is that so? Did you ask him?"

The long pause guts me, bringing to light my short-comings that might always be there. "No. I just know he won't like them. I can wait tables. It's fine."

"It's not fine. My little sister isn't destined for a bland, fine life. You are brave, my dear."

I glance down at my shoes. "Maybe I'm not. Maybe I'm vanilla."

The doom in my own words hits my chest, splintering my ribs with self-condemnation that weights my soul.

I don't believe in myself.

I expect judgment to fill my ears, but instead it's love that greets me. "Hold on, honey cake. I'm coming."

"Huh?"

I don't expect for Winifred to round the corner of the Italian eatery with her phone pressed to her ear. I *really* don't expect for Karen and Agnes to come behind her, heroic grins beaming on their faces.

Winifred marches right up to me, grips both my shoulders and fixes me with a hard stare. "Nobody gets to call my little sister 'vanilla'—not even you." Then she opens the passenger's side of my car and nods for Agnes to grab the box. "Excuse me. We've got an empire to build." Winifred jerks her chin from Karen toward me. "Karen, you look positively feeble, dear. Charlotte, be a darling and give Karen your arm to lean on."

I don't think twice as I extend my arm. "Here, Karen. Are you okay?" But as I take in her pallor, she looks steadier than I feel.

It's not until we reach the entrance of the Spaghetti Scarf that I realize I have been conned. Karen didn't need me to lean on; she was my guide, not I, hers.

A protest bubbles in my throat but I swallow it down. I am supposed to be Charlotte the Brave, not Charlotte the chicken with vanilla cupcakes in her car.

Winifred squares her shoulders and tilts up her chin. "We're here to see Robert." She says it with all the boldness of a warrior storming the enemy's kingdom. I half expect her to mount a horse and pull out a sword.

Or an axe.

The hostess trots off and returns with Robert, who is wiping his hands on a towel.

Instead of greeting me, his eyes fix on my aunt. "Winifred," he says in manner so cold; my spine stiffens.

Aunt Winnie lifts her chin, daring him to have a problem with her. "Hello, Robert. Good to see you."

Robert grumbles, making it clear he does not echo the polite sentiment. I guess he wasn't hoping Winifred would be his new mommy.

His demeanor shifts when his eyes light on me. "Oh, yes. Hello... um... Forgive me. I don't recall your name. I remember the cupcake, but not the name."

I curtsey, and inwardly groan at myself for doing something so formal and stupid. "Charlotte, sir. I brought you a sampling to try for your menu."

His eyebrow quirks at my inept curtsey, no doubt wondering if I hit my head on the way here. "Yes, that's fine. Come on back. I'll call Roberta up. She will want to try them, no doubt. She has more of a sweet tooth than I do." He chuckles to himself. "My boring tastes are probably why the desserts in this place don't sell well."

We exchange pleasant smiles while I try to keep my knees from visibly shaking. Robert disappears into the kitchen, leaving me and my three elderly bodyguards at the hostess stand.

Karen's hand rests on my shoulder while Agnes stands at my side, fixing her fingers to my wrist. "Steady, woman," she urges.

I love that they aren't telling me to simply get over my anxiety. They are taking me seriously, filling in the gaps where my tenacity falls short. Even though I was more than willing to let myself fail on pursuing my dream, they are not.

It is for this reason I decide that I love them—lawbreakers or not.

Robert comes out and escorts us to a table off to the side, laden with a stack of small plates, two glasses of water and a knife.

Robert is all business, but when Roberta rounds the corner and lays eyes on me, she is pure emotion. "Charlotte! My sweet angel. Robert tells me you brought us some desserts to try."

Agnes kisses Roberta on the cheek and sits down beside the woman. No one is about to tell her she is being presumptuous in taking Robert's chair. Robert simply goes and fetches another for himself while Winifred and Karen stand by my sides like sentries.

My hands are trembling as I plate the first cupcake, hoping I don't drop the thing and ruin my chances due to sheer clumsiness.

That would be just my luck.

Robert rubs his palms together. "What are we eating first? A chocolate cupcake, right?"

I nod, wondering if I am allowed to correct him. "It's a chocolate cinnamon cake with a chocolate salted caramel buttercream."

Or, you know, a chocolate cupcake.

Watching two people eat is nerve-racking. I fight the urge to bite my nails as they take their first bite together. When the inhale, the exhale, the closed eyes and the "mm" noises fill the back end of the eatery, my spirits begin to lift. My anxiety untethers itself from my spine and a smile finds my lips.

Next is the lime verbena.

Then the coffee cupcake with dulce de leche Italian meringue.

The fourth is the one I am most nervous about, but given that they have loved and raved about the previous three, I go out on a limb and try my hand at believing this might actually work out for the best.

Just when I am about to introduce the last cupcake flavor, Marianne runs into the restaurant, whips her head around and dashes toward us. I'm expecting her to report a five-alarm fire at the library, but instead she says, "Did I miss it? I tried to get here as soon as I could."

My entire being moves toward her. Without caring about decorum or professionalism, I throw my arms around my friend, grateful for all that she is to me. "You're just in time."

"Whew! The one day people want to go to the library and take their sweet time." Her eyes fix on the table and she deflates. "I did miss it!"

"No, no. They still have one cupcake left."

Karen grins at Roberta. "The best cupcake. We vetted it last night to be sure."

Winifred raises her chin, daring anyone to question

her. "Anyone would be a fool not to buy a dozen on the spot."

Robert is none too pleased with my cheering section, but Roberta grins at all five of us. She clasps her hands together. "Let me guess, this one is vanilla, right?"

I chew on my lower lip, debating again whether or not to correct her.

Marianne has no such qualms. "Actually, it's a vanilla bean cake with a vanilla bean cardamom glaze, topped with Italian meringue that was made with vanilla bean and cardamom sugar."

"Impressive memory," I compliment Marianne, linking my arm through hers.

Her spine lengthens. "Well, I should hope so. I am your dishwasher, after all."

I want this so badly. Even more, I want Robert and Roberta to love this odd flavor I have concocted. In my childish heart, I know that if they love this cupcake, then maybe there might be a place for me here in Sweetwater Falls after all.

Even though she has sampled three cupcakes so far, Roberta finishes her entire portion. She leans back in her chair, sucking on her finger to get the last morsel off. "Oh, Robert. If you don't sell these cupcakes here, you're dead to me."

Robert chuckles, but pushes the rest of his

vanilla cardamom cupcake away after one bite. "Alright, alright. You heard the lady. I would be happy to add the first three to the menu. The fourth one is too weird. The others are good, though."

His verdict sends me simultaneously soaring and then crashing.

Too weird?

I take a breath and decide to take it as a win. I mean, he wants to sell three of my cupcake varieties. I wanted to sell my desserts at a restaurant, and I am getting exactly that opportunity.

I knew the cardamom was too out there for them. Maybe my palette is off.

Too weird.

Robert's critique is a gong in my ears.

Marianne jumps up and down, squealing her excitement.

Winifred's jaw tightens at my mild upset, but she takes the win, as I do. "Very well. Let's talk terms."

I love that she is a pit bull, determined not to let me shake on a raw deal.

However, it is clear that Robert does not like it when Winifred speaks at all. His jaw tightens and his upper lip hints at a curl.

Agnes takes over, holding up her finger. "Three

times the price of the cost to make each batch, minimum. More if you want exclusivity."

My heart nearly stops. I open my mouth to backpedal, but Karen's wink in my direction stills my protest.

Robert leans back in his chair, squinting one eye at Agnes. "What makes you think I would ever agree to something like that?"

Agnes folds her fingers over her midsection. "I helped you study for your economics final, young man. I know what's standard, enough to not get fleeced."

Robert grumbles, and I can feel the deal slipping through my fingers.

Marianne holds tight to my hand, unwilling to let me waver now. "Steady," she whispers.

Robert glares at me. "How much does it cost to make a dozen, young lady?"

I rattle off the exact amount.

Robert scoffs at Agnes. "You realize I would have to charge at least four dollars and fifty cents per cupcake to make a profit."

Agnes leans over and pats him on the head in the most cutely patronizing way one can do such a thing. "Don't forget about the exclusivity bonus. I would charge five dollars even, if I were you." Then she pinches the saggy skin on his cheek. "You did such a good job in that Economics class. A solid C-average, if my memory suffices."

His expression mutates to horror that she remembers his shortcomings so accurately. "Yes, well, fine. You can have your asking price, plus the exclusivity bonus. I'll draw up an agreement and we'll see how it goes." Then he points a scolding finger in my direction. "This is a trial run, understood? I'll give these things thirty days to see if they sell. If not, no harm no foul. Done."

I nod so quickly, I am certain it looks like my eyes are rattling in my head. "Absolutely, sir. You won't be sorry."

Maybe I do belong in Sweetwater Falls after all.

16

SPAGHETTI SCARF CUPCAKES

*R*oberta slides her husband's leftover vanilla cardamom cupcake over to herself and munches on the rest of it. I am slightly mollified that even though my creation was too weird for Robert, at least it struck home with his wife.

Robert stands and waves for me to follow him. "Let's hammer out the details in my office. Just you, not your groupies."

Winifred kisses my cheek. "I'm proud of you, Charlotte. We're going to head out. See you at home."

"Thank you," I tell her, though there are a great many things to which my gratitude could apply.

Aunt Winnie doesn't need to hear any of it. She squeezes my hand, and the four women I adore exit the Spaghetti Scarf.

I trail after Robert, going through the long, narrow kitchen. Notes of garlic, shallots and tomato sauce hit my senses. The tomato is so strong that I scarcely remember any other smell exists.

A pot of water boils on the stove, and is dangerously close to boiling over. The chef stirs a sauce with vigor, splattering a bit of the tomato on the black backsplash. There is no attempt at wiping down the mess as she plates the vibrant sauce over a nest of spaghetti noodles.

A meager row of sharp knives hangs on a magnetic strip across backsplash. The chef yanks one down and hacks into a cooked and ready polish sausage, making me wonder when the last time was that I treated myself to a luscious dinner of sausage and peppers.

It's the wrong knife she's using. Cutting it like that is truly butchering a perfectly delicious sausage. You want the clean cuts on the bias, but the serrated one she is using leaves traces of the innards on the edges of the casing.

The chef frowns at the sausage, as if thinking the same thing.

The aroma is incredible—imperfect cuts or not. I am instantly starving, dying for a plate of pasta.

Robert and I turn left toward a small office littered with piles of paperwork. There is nowhere to sit, including the chair I would think he uses on a regular basis. A cup of coffee sits precariously atop a stack of folders, daring someone to come along and knock it onto the paperwork.

Random words catch my eyes: "Dear Gerald Forbine, I was hoping you might reconsider and sell me the restaurant." There seem to be several like that, all pushed into the same area on Robert's desk. Then there is a pile of what look like legal forms, I'm guessing all to do with Gerald's recent passing.

Robert gestures to the mess. "When you die, make sure you don't dump the paperwork on your child. Unless you hate your son, in which case, this is the perfect revenge."

It's an odd choice of words, to be sure.

I tilt my head to the side. "You two didn't get along?"

Robert searches for a pen and an unused piece of paper. "Oh, we were just about as different as two people can be. Didn't see eye to eye on how the business should be run. I think he lost sight of what made this place special to my mom before she passed. She was always trying new recipes, but when she died, he refused to change a thing." He points at me. "You're lucky you came along when you did. Had you pitched your cupcakes a month ago, you would have had my dad to deal with. He never would have let a new idea like this in."

"I'm grateful for the opportunity." Why does my voice sound squeaky and weird?

I don't want to know about their squabbles. I shouldn't have pried.

Yet, here I go again.

I point to a paper that caught my eye. "He didn't want to sell the restaurant. You did?"

Robert frowns and follows my gaze.

He snatches up the paper as if that will make it disappear from my memory. "That's neither here nor there. I make the business decisions now. This place is legally mine to do with as I please. I'm weighing my options." He jots down a few numbers on a piece of paper. "You should be glad it's me at the wheel. This partnership never would have happened otherwise." His face sours. "Well, maybe it could have. Your aunt had her hooks in my father. She probably could have done a number on him. Bewitched him to throw away all his ideals, as usual."

I grimace at Robert's bitter tone. "Bewitched?"

He seems to recall that I am Winifred's family member, and therefore, less likely to enjoy resentful gossip about my aunt. He fakes a cough and clears his throat a few times, as if that might make me dismiss his rude assessment of my aunt. "I'm fine with starting this on Monday next week. That work for you?"

I nod, but I am still stuck on his assessment of Gerald and Winifred. "You think Winifred made your father throw away his ideals?"

It's clear Robert doesn't want to get into the subject he brought up, but there is no deft way to sidestep a direct question. He swipes his hand across his mustache and fixes me with a hard stare. "My father hadn't dated anyone since my mother died. The day after the ten-year anniversary of her death, he asked Winifred out on a date. Bewitched." He nods once, as if that seals it.

"Maybe your dad was lonely. After ten years..."

Robert slams his hand down on a stack of papers, startling me so much that I let out a small squeak. "My mother was a saint, do you hear me? She never did an irresponsible thing in her life. Dad taking up with anyone is a shock, but Winifred? One of the three members of that ridiculous Live Forever Club? She's trouble, and little else." Light flickers in his eyes, as if a new idea has just occurred to him. "In fact, I wouldn't be surprised if she was the one who killed my father."

Even though I have thought the exact same thing, I back up in horror at the venom and borderline delight in Robert's tone. He has no evidence, only a hatred for my aunt. I don't like being in the same room with this revelation he is having. I feel dirty breathing the same air as him.

I hold up my hands in surrender to his swinging temper. "I'll drop off the first delivery on Monday morning."

Robert seems to understand that this is a conversation in which I will not participate. "A dozen of each flavor. The three good flavors, not that last one. If they sell out, we'll see about upping the shipment."

"Yes, sir." I mumble something that is supposed to communicate "Have a nice day," and also, "Don't talk to me anymore." I turn and march out the door.

I'm indignant and also ashamed that I often entertain a similar guilty verdict about my carefree aunt.

I pass the chef on the way out, giving her a polite nod.

She hacks into a head of cabbage that rests next to a dozen or so carrots. Again, she is using the wrong knife. A steak knife instead of a chef's knife will take twice as long to process the cabbage.

I'm butting in. I realize it. I'm being nosy and pushy when I should just leave with my irritation and a bit of my dignity intact.

However, I cannot help myself. "Excuse me, what are you making?"

Her round face is sweaty, and I can tell she is unenthused at my interruption. "Apple coleslaw."

"That sounds delicious. Do you have a chef's knife?

That might make things easier on you. I can tell you work very hard back here. The whole place smells incredible, thanks to you."

When her eyes tear up, it is clear she hasn't had a compliment in far too long. "Thank you for saying that. These are all Gerald's wife's recipes. I've been working here for twelve years, following them exactly. It's a struggle doing things with the wrong knife. I ordered a new one to replace the one that went missing, but my supplier is behind." She motions to the steak knife. "Thus, I am behind."

I want to hug the struggling woman. She looks to be in her fifties, her dark hair matted to her forehead by the hairnet. Her round face is red and sweaty, her small pink nose moist with either emotion or exhaustion, I cannot tell.

"I'm Charlotte," I offer, though I don't shake her hand, since she is wearing kitchen gloves. "I'll be dropping off cupcakes to add to your menu, so you might see me around more often." I chew on my lower lip, hoping not to seem too eager to befriend the woman. "Can I help? I can deal with the cabbage, if you like. I used to do salad prep at the restaurant I worked at before I moved here."

"Really?" She looks around, mildly concerned. "I

probably shouldn't, but my sus chef called off today, so I'm drowning."

"Happy to help."

The chef sets down the steak knife and bustles to the oven, tugging out a tray of long loaves of bread. "I'm Helen. You're Winifred's niece, right? The new girl."

"I am. That's my full title, too. Charlotte: Winifred's niece, the new girl." I smile at her and pick up the steak knife, wondering how Helen has been keeping her cool with only this and a few other steak knives as her cutting tools.

"Glad to have the help."

Helen wastes no time slathering the bread that's been previously sliced lengthwise with a butter concoction. It smells like pure love and garlic.

"Oh, that smells heavenly."

Helen chuckles. "It does, doesn't it. It was even better last month, if you can believe it. Gerald and the late Mrs. Forbine never tolerated skimping on fresh ingredients. I made the dough myself the night before, and then my sus chef would bake it in the morning." She frowns at the bread on the oven tray before her. "This stuff came to us from a bakery out of town. It's okay, but it's not what it should be."

My mouth pulls to the side while I chop the cabbage

into long strips. "Huh. I would have thought Robert would be all about honoring his mother's memory."

"He is, until he sees a way to save a shiny nickel. Then you'd better hold onto your hat. Robert is always trying to cut corners, but Gerald wouldn't hear of it. The recipe needed to stay the same, even when the cost of produce went up. Now that Gerald is gone?" Helen shakes her head as she hurries to the fridge and pulls out a container. "The quality has already started to go downhill, and Gerald has barely been in the ground for a blink, may he rest in peace. Poor man. To be murdered, not just die? It's awful. I'm sure I should protest this dry loaf of bread more than I did, but I'm too heartbroken to put up much of a fight. The place isn't the same without Gerald."

I finish slicing the cabbage. Then I locate the apples on the counter and begin processing those. We let a few beats of silence settle, so Helen can work while she unburdens herself of a portion of her grief.

"I never met Gerald," I admit. I've been trying to piece together details of him to make a whole picture in my mind. I am hoping it might replace the mental image of his bloated corpse. "It sounds like he was a good boss."

"The best. When I had to have knee surgery, he wouldn't hear of me coming back until my doctor gave me a clean bill of health. Gave me paid leave the entire time, too." Helen's eyes mist over. "Only a good man does something like that." She shakes her head. "He's with his wife now. He's happy."

After I finish slicing the apples, I migrate to Helen, pausing her fluster in the kitchen so I can wrap my arms around her. I don't have true words of comfort, only sympathy. "I'm sorry your friend died."

At this, Helen blubbers on my shoulder, holding on to me—a stranger—because her grief can't be held at bay another moment.

I hold tight to Helen, knowing that I cannot let Gerald's killer go free. If the sheriff hasn't narrowed down his search yet, then I need to step up and figure this out.

Helen deserves closure.

Sweetwater Falls has suffered enough.

17

SPAGHETTI MESS

*I*t is poor form to frequent a dead man's restaurant for the sole purpose of digging into his death, but I guess that is the kind of girl I am this week. Marianne has been a trooper, so I decide to treat her to a meal at the Spaghetti Scarf.

"You don't have to do this," she says, as if no one has ever taken her out before. She spreads her black cloth napkin over her lap.

"You deserve it. You've washed about a hundred dishes to help me out."

"Only a hundred?" she teases. Then her neck shrinks. "I haven't been here since..." She mimes stabbing herself in the chest.

"Since Gerald died?"

She nods and takes out the menu, scouring the items line by line. "I hope the food still tastes the same."

"The bread is different, but so far, Helen has been holding her ground, not letting Robert change the sauces."

Helen and I had many a long chat while I filled in for her sus chef. I can trust the spaghetti to be Gerald's late wife's recipe, but I am not going near the garlic bread out of loyalty to Helen's righteous indignation. After having her handmade bread dethroned by the store-bought stuff, I wouldn't dare order a slice.

"Good to know. Their sauce is classic."

My finger runs down the words on the menu. "I thought it would be good to come here because I need to know if my cupcakes fit well on the menu. They've sold out every day this week, so I'm going to pitch Robert a fourth flavor, but I want to really nail it this time."

Marianne's head bobs, now looking at the menu as if studying for an exam. "I don't suppose a tomato flavor would work."

I grin at her. "I can make anything work in a cupcake. The problem is getting people to buy it. Would you order a tomato cupcake?"

Marianne's face pulls. "Ugh. No. Though, I'm sure if you made it, I would love it."

We giggle together because our friendship lends itself to levity and contentment. It's easy being with Marianne. I don't know how I lasted so long without a solid girlfriend before this.

I order the apple slaw and the spaghetti bolognaise, because I happen to know the apple slaw is fabulous. "What are you reading now?" I ask Marianne, knowing she plows through a classic every few days.

Marianne's smile when she talks about literature is simply adorable. Her exhale as she tosses her braid over her shoulder makes her look as if she is ready to write sonnets about her passion.

She sets down her menu as if she has freshly fallen in love and must divulge every sordid detail. "Mm. I'm reading *Pride and Prejudice* again. I keep thinking I've read it enough times to memorize the thing, but it never gets old. Every time I read it, it's like the first time all over again."

"Sounds like you love the story. I've never read it," I admit.

I can tell this is the wrong thing to say.

She leans forward, palms slapped to the table. "What? Are you serious?"

I shoot her a wry look. "You're acting like I've just told you I'm illiterate and use book pages as toilet paper. I read. I just haven't read *Pride and Prejudice*."

Marianne moves her hands around until both palms settle atop the table again. "I'll plow through and finish it tonight. Then it's yours."

"I don't have a library card yet." I snicker at her sudden seriousness.

"Sure you do. Or you will, anyway. I'll start one for you tomorrow."

"Marianne, honestly, I can wait. I..."

I have no idea what I am about to say because at that exact moment, the one person I truly don't want to see comes into the restaurant, accompanied by a woman who is possibly his mother.

Strong jawline, long but not too prominent nose, sandy hair done perfectly, and an easy way about them both that suggests they know what they are doing in life.

"We have to leave!" I whisper, reaching for my purse. "I'll take you somewhere else."

But of course, that is the moment when the waiter sets our drinks down.

Marianne tilts her head at my odd shift in personality, and then gives the waiter her order.

"And you, Miss?"

I rattle off my order, tripping over the easy words as if I am a child who has never understood how to hold her poise in a grownup establishment.

When the waiter leaves, I am sweating. "We have to go!"

Marianne looks around, her eyes landing on the source of my consternation. "Why? What's wrong?"

"It's him! That guy over there. He's so beautiful, he turns me into a klutz if I'm near him for too long. I shouldn't be in the same restaurant as him."

"Who, Logan?" She says the name as if she cannot believe how crazy it sounds that anyone would have a fangirl crush on him. I mean, the man could pass for a calendar model of handymen or sweater models.

"Yes! Don't say his name. He'll know I'm talking about him." I shake my head too quickly. I'm sure I look like a caricature. "We have to get out of here. Why did I order?"

Marianne snickers at me. "Your face is completely red. Have you met Logan before?"

I hang my head in shame as the embarrassing story of the grocery store catastrophe lays itself out for her.

Marianne is laughing so hard by the end of my pathetic story that there is no way Logan doesn't see us.

I angle my chair so I can't see him at his table across the restaurant. If I could will myself to become invisible, I would do so right now.

"And you fell into his arms? That's so sweet! I love it." Marianne claps at my ineptitude.

"It wasn't sweet. It was horrible! I don't want a guy like that to know I exist. And I *really* don't want him to meet me when I'm splattered in pickled egg juice."

Marianne covers her mouth, but her giggles cannot be masked. "Oh, that's excellent. Poor Charlotte. I'm sure he thought it was all very funny."

"Yes. Hilarious. My mortification is amusing to the hot guy. Awesome." I plop both elbows on the table and cradle my forehead in my palms.

After a little more teasing, Marianne finally switches her focus back to books. I love listening to her gush about the plot, telling which twists and turns are her favorite. Her whimsy is just distracting enough that, for a few minutes, I forget about Logan.

When the waiter comes with our food, I am struck by the vibrancy of the sauce. It isn't the typical red, but a brighter hue that makes me think orange tomatoes were added into the mix. Maybe even carrots.

I inhale over my food, knowing this is going to be a good meal. I mean, Helen made it, so I am certain I will enjoy it.

"Are you sure you'll have enough time to help me with the twinkle lights set up?" Marianne starts cutting into her stuffed cannelloni. "I mean, you're working at the diner, plus baking when you get off your shift. I don't want to steal your one free day."

"Stealing me to hang out and play in twinkle lights is the only kind of thievery I will never oppose."

I twirl my fork in the noodles, readying for what I assume will be the best bite of my week.

The flavor is incredible. Fresh tomatoes pop on my tongue, reminding me that summer can be felt year-round if only you have a solid cook to remind you of nature's best assets. The nest of crispy, caramelized onions on top is my favorite part—both the smell and the taste.

"Hi, Marianne. Haven't seen you in a while. How are you?"

The velvety voice sets my nerves on edge because there is only one man who could sound so very alluring.

Marianne lights up with a knowing grin that aims a bit of its tease my way. "Hey, Logan. I'm reading *Pride and Prejudice*, so life is pretty good. How about you?"

If my face was red before, I am certain it is purple now. I refuse to look up. I don't want to see how pretty he is. Not up close.

"I'm not reading anything that interesting. Just reports and boring stuff like that." When his voice angles my way, I will myself to evaporate into thin air. "Hello, Charlotte."

He deserves more than a bob of my head, but when I

open my mouth to say hello, I forget my mouthful of spaghetti that isn't quite chewed yet.

A sharp inhale of nerves drags noodles, some meat and sauce down the wrong pipe...

...and gets stuck.

My eyes water as I choke on the meat. My whole body seizes from both embarrassment and horror. My hand grips the table as I fish for my napkin. If I die of spaghetti ingestion, it's suddenly very important to me that I don't make a mess in front of Logan.

Both Logan and Marianne are trying to coach me through my next breath, but it looms just out of reach.

Marianne jumps out of her seat and rounds the table, but Logan is closer and reaches me first. I want to apologize and run for the door, but I can't muster the wherewithal to stand on my own, even when he yanks me out of my seat.

Logan's arms encircle my waist just below my ribs, my spine pressed to his chest.

My arm flails and catches on the edge of my plate, dumping my spaghetti on my arm and hand. The burning sensation is nothing to the flush of heat I feel from Logan's arms wrapped around me from behind. Even as I am fighting for breath, I cannot help but think how wonderful his arms feel.

If this is the last embrace before I die, it will have been a good one.

Logan pushes his fist to my diaphragm three times before the lodged chunk of meat projectiles out of my mouth and onto the table.

I don't know if it's the handsome man still holding me from behind or if it's the loss of oxygen, but my knees are ready to give out.

Logan lowers me to my chair as our waiter scurries around us, fanning a menu at me and chanting over and over for me to breathe.

Marianne has moisture on her cheeks. I scared her.

I scared myself.

Marianne dabs at my mouth with a napkin. "Oh, honey. Are you okay?"

Logan holds onto my hand as if he has no idea what such contact does to a woman.

I manage a wan nod, my chest heaving as I reacquaint myself with the effort of breathing.

Logan chuckles at himself. "A mishap for each time I've seen you. I'm starting to think I might be bad luck for you."

He hit it right on the nose. Someone of his cuteness caliber will only ever be bad luck for me.

Marianne's arms find their way around me while the

waiter switches from panicked to relieved to now irritated that he has to clean up my meal, which has been dumped all over the floor.

The waiter cannot possibly hate me more than I loathe myself right now.

18

CLOSING UP

*L*ogan's long fingers span across my back, rubbing in a soothing circle. Of course he is the sort of man who knows CPR and can be kind to a dolt like myself, who hasn't yet learned how to chew properly.

"Home," I beg Marianne, who quickly obliges. She asks the waiter to box up the remnants of our food, and chats with Logan as if talking to the most handsome man in the world is easy.

"You have to try the cupcakes," Marianne prods Logan after a few back and forths, wherein I try to even out my breathing. "Charlotte made them."

"No kidding. Then I guess I don't have a choice. So long as they don't have pickled eggs in them, I'm sold."

He's trying to make a joke, to be friendly, but I can't

muster up an ounce of levity. I'm still sitting in my seat, my hand still dripping with spaghetti sauce.

I wish I hadn't made such an epic fool of myself.

In my imagination, I would happen to come across Logan at random. I would say something witty and toss my hair over my shoulder, fixing him with a clever grin.

I would not be a mess of bright sauce and projectile meat.

"Bathroom," I mumble while the waiter goes off to get a box for Marianne's food.

When Logan helps me to stand, I realize the entire restaurant is gaping at me, including Logan's mother, her hand over her mouth.

Pity. That's what I see in her eyes, as well as in all the other patrons, who are looking on with concern.

I gently pull away from Logan with as much dignity as I have left, which admittedly, isn't much. "Thank you," I whisper, my voice hoarse. "Thank you for saving my life."

Logan fixes me with the beginnings of half a smile. "Any time."

Yep. He's too handsome.

I stumble to the bathroom with Marianne by my side, grateful when the door closes his beauty out of sight. "That was horrible!" I squawk, only now getting my voice back. "I told you, I can't be near someone that good looking. It's a hazard."

"Apparently." She shakes her head at me. "You weren't kidding. Here, honey. Let's clean you up." Marianne turns on the spray of cold water, cooling my skin as I try to scrub the sauce off my hands and arms.

I chastise myself through gritted teeth while I scrub. "If that's not the way to leave a lasting impression, I don't know what is. I will forever be the hapless, hopeless girl who can't get through a meal without choking on it if Logan is near."

"You've got it bad, that's for sure." She tries to hide her chuckle, ironing out her smile and then shaking her head. "It's not funny. You choked. That was scary."

I frown at her. "It's not funny or scary. It's stupid. You have to keep me away from him, or I'll cause some real problems for myself."

Marianne screws her lips together. I can tell she is teetering between worry over me almost choking to death, and hilarity because, well, I am terrible around handsome men.

Actually, that's not completely true. "I don't usually get that bad. My clumsiness worsens as the guy gets more handsome. If Logan was only pretty good looking, this wouldn't be a problem." Butterflies flutter in my belly when his face comes into my imagination. "He's the kind of pretty that photographers only dream about. He's the kind of gorgeous that makes a girl forget that a man should also have a good personality, which, judging by the fact that he just saved my life, he probably does." I'm flustered as I scrub my hands to no avail. The color is sticking stubbornly to my fingers and forearm. "He's the sort of beautiful that should come with a warning label."

Marianne gives up the fight with decorum and lets out a loud laugh. "I'm sorry! It's just that I've never seen anyone react so strongly to anyone, much less Logan."

I narrow my eyes at her as I pump more soap into my palm. The sauce is stubborn, the pigment sticking to my skin even though I am finally clean. "I prefer to crush on someone from afar, not have him be in the same restaurant as me!" I growl at the stains on my hands. No matter how hard I scrub, it's still clear that I went up against a plate of spaghetti and lost.

Marianne's laughter stills, her face frozen and her smile twisted in what looks like alarm.

"What?"

"Charlotte, look." She points at my hands in horror.

"I know, I've scrubbed them three times over, and they're still orange."

"No, Charlotte. Your hands are *orange*."

I look again, my brain struggling to push through my mortification to see what is right in front of me.

Finally the facts line themselves up, each one slamming in my chest using a force with which I cannot contend.

"Gerald's hands and arms were orange when I found him." The second I say it aloud, I know I need to verify my theory before it can stick in my mind.

I race out of the bathroom, banging straight into none other than Logan.

I wobble on my feet at the contact combined with having slammed into the most perfect human on the planet.

"Whoa! Sorry, Charlotte." Logan's hands cup my shoulders. "I was waiting to see if you were alright."

I try not to look into his bright green eyes. It's like staring directly into the sun. Still, I manage to form a semi-coherent thought and notice the glimpse of laughter in his eyes beneath the concern.

My mouth firms. "You overheard me, didn't you."

Logan holds up his hands. I'll bet the man has never told a lie in his life. "I didn't mean to. I really did just come to see if you were alright." The corner of his mouth crooks upward. "You really think I'm pretty?"

Obviously. I also think the world is round.

The urge to vomit overwhelms me. I am overtaken

with mortification and horror. How do I manage to do the exact wrong thing every time I am near this man?

"Excuse me!" I shield my hand over my eyes and duck my head, rushing by him to escape his presence.

Besides, I've got a hunch to check on.

I burst into the kitchen with all the gusto of one declaring war. "Helen?" I call, and start trotting through the long, narrow kitchen. Each step away from Logan helps me regain my sense of normalcy.

Helen pops her head up from the other side of the island. "Charlotte, are you alright?"

"Maybe." I point to her hands. "Why do you wear those gloves?"

She quirks an eyebrow at me. "Because if I didn't, it would be a health violation?"

Duh.

"No other reason?"

Helen tilts her head to the side, fixing me with a stare of curiosity. "Well, if I didn't, my hands would look like yours." Her shoulders vibrate with mirth as she points to my discolored hands and wrists.

"What about Gerald? Did he ever cook back here with you?"

Helen's eyes flash with hurt. I hate that I am bringing this up. "Of course. He was a good owner. He always wore gloves because he knew if he didn't, his hands would wind up like yours. Also, you know, it's a health violation not to."

"He always wore them in the kitchen? What about if he was here by himself?"

Helen screws her face in confusion. "He has never had orange dying his skin. Never would. We put carrots in the sauce. He's no fool. We wear the gloves for the public's safety, but also to protect our skin."

"When was the last time you saw him?"

Helen's voice catches. "The day before his body was found. That afternoon."

So Winifred wasn't the last person to see Gerald alive.

My heart soars at the news.

"And his hands were normal? Not stained with the sauce?"

Helen rounds the stainless steel island and fixes her hands on her hips. "Not a drop. Like I said, he always wore gloves. What's this about?"

At that exact moment, Marianne bursts into the kitchen, her hands over her eyes. "I'm not supposed to be in here!" she announces.

I start puzzling out the itch in my brain aloud. "When I found Gerald's body, his hands and arms were orange. I thought it was paint, but it could have been the sauce."

Helen shrugs. "It's possible he had his gloves off and some sauce spilled on his hands. You can ask Robert. He closed up with his dad that night."

My reply comes out slow. "I don't think that's true. Robert didn't see his father the day Gerald died."

As if summoned by the sound of his own name, Robert walks out of his office and stands in the kitchen. His eyes narrow, taking in my frozen body language. "What are we talking about, ladies?" He wears the tone of a teacher who caught me whispering in class.

Helen is too busy tending to the tomatoes to take in the shifting tenor of the room. "The girls were saying that Gerald didn't see you the night before his body was found, but that's not true. You were with him. Did he spill sauce on his hands when you two were here? They're saying he was found with orange on his hands. Probably from the sauce."

Robert doesn't take his eyes off me. It's like he is trying to sift through my brain, picking out accusations I might hurl at him before they can birth from my lips. "Is that so? I couldn't say."

Be brave. Be brave. Be brave.

"Couldn't say if Gerald had sauce on his hands, or couldn't say that you were here the night of his murder?"

Robert draws himself up, claiming every inch of his

superior height. "I have a business to run. You can see yourselves out."

"Sure thing." I force my voice to sound chipper. "I need to check on my cupcake shipment before I go. They were looking a little frosty. Maybe they should go on a lower shelf in the cooler." I motion for Helen to show me where she stores the cupcakes I sent in, but Robert steps toward me, his mouth firm with displeasure.

Marianne beelines toward him. "Robert, quick question. What makes the sauce stain? Charlotte got some on her hands, and we can't get it out."

It's an innocuous question, but it derails him just long enough for me to steal a few seconds with Helen in the cooler.

My voice is surprisingly calm and quiet as I pretend to inspect my cupcakes. "Robert told the police that he didn't see his dad the day of Gerald's death."

Helen takes a step back, clearly afraid of her own words. "But I saw them together. They were bickering, as usual. They were getting on my nerves, so Gerald told me he would clean up the kitchen for me with Robert." Her lower lip quivers. "I never saw Gerald again."

Though I can tell Marianne is running out of chatter, I steal a few seconds and gather up Helen in a hearty hug. I take the opportunity to whisper a warning in her ear. "Careful. Don't bring any of this up with him again. I'll take care of it." I kiss Helen's plump cheek. "You may not be able to see Gerald again, but you are helping solve his murder. That's a great gift to give a friend."

Helen stiffens. "What?"

I whirl around and grab Marianne by the hand, practically tugging her out the door. "The cupcakes look great! See you when I bring in the next shipment."

Now I am positive I know who did it.

I only have to prove it to someone who can actually do something about it.

19

OFFICER FLOWERS

I have never been to the Sweetwater Falls Police Station in the daylight before. Then again, I haven't visited most of the places this town has to offer.

I study every angle of the building, impatient because apparently, the sheriff's office around here is an answering machine when the sun sets.

I sat on this information all night, which didn't exactly make for a pleasant sleep. Aunt Winifred made me a cup of chamomile tea, but it did nothing to settle my nerves. When dawn hit, I showered and dressed in my most responsible outfit: a navy pencil skirt and fitted sage blouse with my most formidable heels.

Now I'm sitting in Winifred's golf cart, waiting with my aunt for the precinct to finally open.

I mean business today. I am not about to shirk away from this mission of solving the mystery of Gerald's death. It has to come full circle, or I will never be able to shake the image of his dead body from when I found it atop that pile of compost.

"You're sure about this?" Winifred worries. She hardly ever voices concern, so I know I have pushed her to her limit.

"Sure as I'll ever be."

"You're accusing someone of Gerald's murder. That's not a thing a person can bounce back from if they're wrong."

"I don't know about you, but I don't want a murderer walking free around Sweetwater Falls. We deserve to be safe." I fiddle with my blouse as the warm wind touches my cheeks. "And I'm not wrong."

Her mouth screws to the side. "I still don't believe it."

"That's because I didn't tell you how I got there." I tap my temple. "It makes sense in my head." I hold her gaze with a steadiness I am learning to conjure when I need it. "Charlotte the Brave, right?"

Winifred draws herself up with dignity befitting a queen. "Indeed. Onward, then." We move out of her golf cart and into the precinct, making our way to the intake desk. Aunt Winnie's hand on my back serves to steady my nerves.

Marianne rushes in through the front door, sidestepping the tall fichus in the corner and making a straight line to us. "Nearly missed it. Whew!"

Agnes and Karen are hot on her heels, entering in seconds after my favorite librarian. Each of them greets us with hugs, which is just about the best feeling in the world. If I wasn't on my way to accuse someone of murder, I would think life can't get better than this.

When a figure comes around the corner and stops on the other side of the visitor's desk, my mouth drops open in horror. "You!"

My face flushes red while my body heats up in a way I cannot quell. My feet take several steps back until I bump into Marianne, who is surprisingly unmovable, despite her petite frame.

"Hi, Logan," Marianne says in a chipper yet somehow also serious tone.

If I thought Logan was devastatingly handsome before, it is nothing to how starstruck I am now, standing on the other side of the desk from him.

"I... um... see I... and then... and he..." My words are stuck in my throat, coming out in weird spurts at a higher pitch than I normally can achieve. I cast around for a diversion to get his gaze off of me. "Have to go!" I screech, startling Winifred and Karen.

Agnes, I notice, is sniggering, just like Marianne.

I guess Marianne doesn't keep anything from her big sister—not even my embarrassing crush.

"Oh, no," Agnes insists. "This bright, beautiful, talented, *single* young lady needs to speak with the sheriff."

Would that I could melt into the floor to escape this moment.

Logan's smile is fixed on me. He is so stunning; it's like staring into the sun. My chin tilts to the side, my whole body flinching away from the charm he emanates. His poise clashes horribly with my awkward nature.

"What are you doing here?" I ask in a whisper, as if the act of Logan being in the police station is some sort of scandal.

He points to the badge on his chest. "I think the question is, what are *you* doing here? I work here. Can I help you ladies with anything this morning?"

My eyes zero in on his nametag.

L. Flowers.

"You're Sheriff Flowers' son?" Everything I say comes out as an accusation.

He tilts his head to the side. "Sure am. Going on thirty-five years."

His sandy blond hair takes on a honeyed hue under the fluorescent glow. Only he would still find a way to look appealing in this lighting.

Logan leans forward, his hands pressed to the table. "Can I help you ladies?"

Marianne jerks me forward, countering my instinct to run away. "Charlotte thinks she might know who murdered Gerald."

"Is that so?" comes the sheriff's voice from a few feet behind Logan. "You here to confess, Winifred?"

My aunt stiffens beside me. "Fine. I did it."

Both Flowers men, a woman filing papers toward the back, and all four of us go still.

My heart pounds as the world ceases to make sense. "What?" I ask Winifred.

My aunt throws her hands in the air. "I confess. I did it. I told the entire town that you were a bedwetter, Louis. I know I shouldn't have done it, but you were really getting on my nerves, accusing me of Gerald's death. So I told Delia, and she told everyone."

Karen shakes her head while Agnes starts to giggle. "Well, Delia is the town gossip. No better way to spread the word than to tell her a secret."

Sheriff Flowers lowers his shoulders. "Hilarious. Get in here if you have something useful to add. See yourselves out if you plan on wasting more of my time."

Marianne holds up her hand. "Charlotte has information."

Though, at this point, I'm not sure I can string two sentences together. "Why didn't you tell me Logan worked here?" I whisper to her.

Marianne grins in reply. "Because this is better entertainment for me. Come on, now. I'll go with you."

Heels were the wrong choice. I am no more graceful than a giraffe on stilts as Logan waves us toward the hallway. "Let's go in here and have a chat."

I can't make my feet work. My brain is foggy the nearer Logan is. I came here to have an intelligent discussion, but I am not sure I can work out simple arithmetic at this point.

His physique combined with the uniform is a sight my brain cannot comprehend. I am either going to faint or throw up if he doesn't go away.

Winifred fans me. "Goodness, Charlotte! You're all flushed."

Karen looks Logan up and down as he opens an interrogation room and escorts us inside. "You really think he's that good looking?"

I keel over. "I'm going to be sick."

Logan touches my elbow, and I swear, my vision tunnels. "Are you alright?"

Heat ricochets through my body. My heart hammers so hard and fast; I am certain he can hear the affect he has on my most vital organ.

I shoot away from him. "Oh! You can't touch me like that. It's too much!"

"I'm sorry?" Logan looks truly at a loss.

I put up my hand to block out the sight of his beautiful face, my chin turned to the side. "You're too pretty. We've been over this. If you don't want me to throw up all over this table, send your dad in while you wait outside or something. I'm telling you, I can't, and this is important."

Karen's laughter rings in my ears while Winifred chortles slowly.

Logan's voice is gentle with a heavy tease to it. "You're not serious. I'm not... No one has ever..." He takes a step toward me.

I dash to the corner like a criminal trying to escape the law. "I'm telling you, if you come near me, I will barf on your table!"

It's a strange threat, but oddly effective.

Logan backs up, his hands raised as if I have a gun aimed at his chest. "Okay. Sorry. I didn't mean to..."

Have this face?

Be dressed in a uniform that fits far too perfectly?

Be this gorgeous?

There is no possible way he can finish that sentence.

He makes it to the doorway and pauses, turning

back around to face me. "Miss Charlotte, I'm really not..."

The teasing tone he uses to say my name is not helping matters. At this point, I will never get over my crush.

Marianne bursts into high-pitched laughter. "You heard the lady, Logan! Your face makes her want to vomit."

Winifred pinches his cheek for good measure. "Out you go."

Logan dips his head toward me, his hand over his heart. "I'll send in the sheriff." His voice lowers before he exits. It is laced with a tease that heats my cheeks all over again. "Though, if you develop a crush on my father, I'll be sorely gutted."

I cover my face and tuck my body back into the corner, wishing this whole ordeal could just be over.

When the door opens again, I relax immediately when Sheriff Flowers enters, notebook in hand. "Morning, ladies. Any new crimes I should be aware of?"

Winifred mimes a laugh in his direction and slaps his cheek twice. "My niece thought she would come by and solve Gerald's murder for you. I hope that doesn't throw a wrench in your plans for the day. I know you were hoping to stop by and harass me later."

Sheriff Flowers narrows his eyes at Winifred. "Still

might." He sits down at the table, motioning for me to take the only other seat in the small room. "What have you got for me, city girl?"

My knees are wobbly, otherwise I wouldn't take him up on his offer to sit, especially when there are three elderly women who could probably use a rest.

"I know who killed Gerald, Sheriff Flowers. It wasn't my aunt."

He snorts derisively. "Of course it wasn't. She's innocent as a nun, isn't she."

That hardly describes Winifred.

"It wasn't her because someone else was with him the day after Winnie and Gerald broke up."

My declaration straightens the spines of all three members of the Live Forever Club.

I grip the edge of the table, gearing up to clear my aunt's name, once and for all.

20

THE LAST ONE TO SEE GERALD ALIVE

*W*inifred turns toward me, giving my verdict her full attention. "I don't understand, Charlotte. Someone saw Gerald alive after I ended things with him?"

The interrogation room is cold and unfriendly. There aren't any cheery pictures on the wall, only warnings to make sure you are apprised of the suicide hotline, the proper child car seat weight limits, and the name and number of a lawyer, who apparently can get you the best rates in town.

I shake my head, tugging on my fingers as I begin to lay out the evidence. "We all thought you were the last person to see Gerald, but when I discovered Gerald's body, I noticed one detail that didn't make it into your report."

The sheriff rears back. "And how would you know what's in my report?"

I search rapidly for any explanation that doesn't involve breaking and entering into the police station. "Um..."

Winifred straightens, her hand on my shoulder. "Give her a minute. She's nervous. Your son got her all riled up."

Another look of disbelief from the sheriff. No doubt he is thinking that we are accusing Logan of being a troublemaker, which could not be further from the truth.

After a deep breath, my mind clears. "When you came to our home to interrogate Winifred, you said there was nothing unusual about the body, but there was. Gerald's hands were orange."

The sheriff shrugs, but I can tell my observation makes him uncomfortable. "What of it? Have you ever eaten at the Spaghetti Scarf? You touch your fork, and your fingers are orange for days."

I bite my tongue to keep from telling him that I have, in fact, eaten at the Spaghetti Scarf. His son saved my life there just yesterday.

"Gerald wears gloves," Marianne points out, stepping forward to stand on my other side. Her arms cross over her chest, and in this moment, it is clear to me she does have a streak of wildness to her. "We interviewed Helen yesterday in the kitchen."

Sheriff Flowers shakes his head at us, clearly exasperated that we have taken matters into our own hands. "Of course you did. I assume you have even a smidgen of police training, right?"

I fidget in my seat but refuse to be derailed. "Helen told us that Robert and Gerald were arguing, so she clocked out early. Helen is on her way." I pull out my phone and glance at the time. "She should be here soon to give you her statement. She can confirm that Robert lied about being home that day."

"I'm on the very edge of my seat," the sheriff drones. Though, he does begin writing down notes, so at least there's that.

Agnes' frown takes over her face. "Don't you take that tone with her. And sit up straight, young man. You're at work, not at a back alley for beatniks. You'll end up stooped before your time."

He glowers at Agnes but obeys.

I'll admit, I love the sight of a grown authority figure being bossed by a sweet old woman who knits tea cozies.

Marianne smirks at the phrase "back alley for beatniks," which is objectively hilarious.

I need to stop tugging on my fingers. I know it

projects weakness and nerves, but the truth of the matter is that I am filled with both of those things.

Still, I know there is a streak of bravery in me. When I reach for it, my fingers steady.

I press on to make sure there is no doubt in the sheriff's mind who the killer is. "Helen left work early the night before Gerald's body was found on the compost pile. Gerald was wearing gloves when he was helping her in the kitchen, because he is well aware of how badly the sauce stains. Robert stayed late with Gerald." I draw myself up in my seat, squaring my shoulders to deliver the truth. "Robert lied to you. He is the last person to have seen Gerald alive."

It's a rush to get it all out, and for that span of several seconds, I am proud of myself.

Of course, that confidence leaves me completely when the door opens and Logan Flowers steps inside.

Then I revert back to my nervous self, readying myself to vomit.

HELEN'S HELP

*L*ogan Flowers is captivating in his uniform. I want to tell him to please leave so I can finish my talk with the sheriff, but all intelligent speech leaves me when his clear, bright green eyes settle on my angst-riddled expression.

Though he addresses the room at large, the corner of his mouth drags up, fixing his half-smile on me. "I have Helen here, ready to see you, Sheriff. She would like to give a statement about Gerald's whereabouts the day before his body was discovered."

Logan is no less beautiful than he was mere minutes ago, and I am no less affected by his stunning features. My entire body flushes pink. My chin lowers, my hand shielding my forehead because his beauty is as potent as staring into the sun.

Sheriff Flowers sighs. "Alright, bring her in. Might as well join the party here. Did you know we have a town of sleuths, Logan?"

I glance up just in time to catch Logan's smirk, which is still directed at me. "I know better than to underestimate the women of Sweetwater Falls." Then he swings the door open wider, letting Helen inside the now crowded room.

I hope and expect for Logan to leave, but he snicks the door shut with himself included in the cramped interrogation room.

All the breath sucks out of my lungs. I had so many well thought out points to tell the sheriff, but I can't call upon a single fact. The soft indentation of Logan's chin dimple is too distracting, and apparently requires all of my focus.

Luckily, Marianne has my back. "Helen, tell the sheriff what you told us."

Helen obliges, noting that Gerald was alone with his son at the Spaghetti Scarf the night before the man was found dead. She confirms that Robert was the last person to see Gerald alive.

Gotta love a woman who knows how to tell the truth, because she has nothing nefarious to hide.

The sheriff scribbles on his notepad, taking down every word because it is pure case-cracking gold. He pauses to look up at Helen. "You mentioned they were arguing, so Gerald sent you home. Since Robert lied about being there at all, I highly doubt he'll be forthcoming if I ask what they were arguing about."

Helen shoots me a warning look, and then jerks her head toward Winifred.

Though my brain is partway scrambled because of the beautiful man in the room, I miraculously understand why Helen is hesitant to answer the sheriff's question.

"Logan?" My voice is suddenly dry and quiet, reeking of uncertainty. I think we are both a little surprised that I am addressing him directly.

Bravery. Bravery. Bravery.

"Yes, Miss Charlotte?" Logan replies, his tone laced with a tease.

My heart hammers. I fight as hard as I am able against the crush that threatens to leave me wordless and hapless. "Could you... Could you please... Would you mind taking my aunt for a walk? This is a lot, and she could use some water."

Agnes and Karen snap to life, seeming to understand that whatever Helen is about to say, Winifred should not have to hear it. "Absolutely. That's a great idea, Charlotte," Karen says.

Agnes loops her arm through Winifred's, even

though my aunt does not look certain that she wants to leave the room right in the thick of the action.

Logan dips his chin in my direction, looking like a dashing gentleman about to lay a kiss on a fair maiden's hand. "As you wish, Miss Charlotte." He straightens and proffers his arm to my aunt, completing the picture of civility. "Let me get you some fresh air, Winifred. It's too stuffy in here for me. Plus, I haven't heard your take on whether or not my desk is organized properly. Maybe you can help me with that."

A shiver of attraction rolls through me, noting that his sweetness only makes him more desirable.

I need to get far away from this lovely man, or I will never have another coherent thought for the rest of my days.

Karen and Agnes follow behind, but Agnes turns to wink at me before she shuts her and the rest of the Live Forever Club out of the interrogation room.

Helen's shoulders deflate. "Gerald and Robert were arguing about Winifred. They usually argue about how the business should be run. Gerald wants things to stay the same, while Robert wants to cut corners."

"I see." Sheriff Flowers scrawls a few more sentences on his notepad. "What else can you tell me about the argument?"

Helen swallows hard. I can tell she doesn't like

involving herself in controversy. Still, she knows this is the right thing to do to honor her deceased boss. "Gerald waited ten years after his wife died before dating anyone. Apparently, that was too soon for Robert to accept."

"Tell me more," the sheriff prods.

I take that bit of wisdom and pack it away in my memory. If he wants to know more, he asks for it, then he shuts up.

I can do that.

The sheriff comments little now, only speaking to gain more information. I like that.

Helen wipes her palms off on her shirt, summoning her confidence to come forward with the whole story. "'You're dishonoring Mom's memory, dating anyone at your age. She deserves to rest in peace, knowing no one else has your eye.' It was stuff like that. Robert didn't want his father moving on. Robert is a yeller in the kitchen, and he didn't hold back. Gerald didn't back down, though. He doesn't yell to get his point across, but he's just as stubborn. 'You don't think a decade is long enough? I'm getting on in years, Son. I don't want to live another day with my best days long gone. Winifred makes me laugh. Don't you think I deserve a little laughter?'" Helen shakes her head. "Heartbreaking, the whole thing. I had to get out of there. When it was clear Robert wasn't going to let up, Gerald told me to clock out early, and they would lock up for the night."

When it seems Helen has run out of steam, I guide her to my next bit of evidence. "Helen, are you missing any knives from the kitchen?"

Helen's eyes widen. "Yes, but..." Horror dawns on her features, her mouth popping open in shock. I can tell this is the piece of the puzzle that truly guts her. "Oh, not one of my knives! That sweet man was murdered with my chef's knife?" She cups her mouth, catching a sob that comes out unbidden. She shakes her head, her eyes pooling with moisture. "Oh, Robert. How could you?"

I don't have the stomach to sit down when a woman is crying. Just like when Roberta was upset at the diner, my heart moves my body closer to Helen. My arms curve around her, holding her tight because no one should have to cry alone.

I lock eyes with the sheriff and nod, letting him know I have come to the end of my pitch.

The sheriff's mouth firms as he continues scribbling in his notebook. "Thank you, Helen." He fixes his stare on her anxious state. "You look like you're coming down with the flu."

"Oh, I don't..."

The sheriff interrupts her, but I forgive him instantly

when I hear his reason. "It might be a good idea for you to call in to work and tell them you can't come in. You look like you might have the flu for the next two hours, actually. After that, you'll probably experience a miraculous recovery."

Helen exhales. "Thank you, Sheriff. Come to think of it, I do feel like I've just come down with a two-hour flu."

He smiles at her, which is an expression I did not think him capable of. "Thank you, Helen. I'll take care of it from here."

Helen squeezes me and then moves toward the door. She all but dashes out the exit, no doubt aiming to rush home and lock her doors.

Marianne grips my hand. "Robert killed his father."

The sheriff stands, his few superior inches of height seeming to tower over me. "It seems to be that way. You girls shouldn't have involved yourselves." A small smirk chases on the heels of his mild scolding. "But I'm glad you did."

"Thank you, Sheriff."

The sheriff extends his hand, shaking mine with a firm grip. "Welcome to Sweetwater Falls, Charlotte McKay."

22

ATTACK

*M*arianne and I have all but worn a hole in the living room carpet, pacing back and forth. "We should have heard from Sheriff Flowers by now," I say again.

"You would think we would get an update, at least." Marianne's brow is furrowed in the same immovable way mine has been for the past hour.

Winifred's chamomile tea has done nothing to settle my soul. I need to know that Robert has been locked up. I need to know this whole thing can finally be over. Still, my aunt refills our teacups that rest on the end table by the sofa. "Girls, you're going to make yourselves sick, worrying like this. Sheriff Flowers has it under control." She shakes her head. "I still can't believe it was Robert who killed Gerald. His own father. What is the world coming to?"

Karen calls to Winifred from the kitchen, where she, Agnes and my aunt have been playing cards in silence for the past hour. "Robert is a child who never grew up. All I can hope is that it was an accident, that he didn't actually mean to murder poor Gerald."

Though Winifred was escorted out of the room when Helen divulged that Gerald and Robert had been fighting over whether or not Gerald should be dating Aunt Winnie, it's clear everyone knows that is exactly what the fight was about.

Winifred's hand shakes as she pours the tea. "Murdered with one of his own kitchen knives in his own restaurant? I can't. It's too tragic." She moves back into the kitchen with surprising grace.

"Hey," I say, pointing to my aunt as I follow her into the kitchen. "You're not limping anymore. Did the turmeric tea I got help you?"

Winifred blinks at me, confused at my comment. "That's why you bought the tea? I didn't realize. Honey cake, I don't have joint pain or inflammation. I was limping because of this." She hikes up the hem of her khaki shorts and displays her thigh to the room.

My mouth drops open in time with Marianne's

screech of astonishment. "Is that what I think it is?" Marianne points at the scandal.

Winifred's chin lifts with pride. "It sure is, and it hurt like you wouldn't believe. I always wanted a tattoo, so the day before you moved here, Charlotte, I took the plunge. Do you like it?"

I rub my forehead, taking in the very good reason for her limp. I can't believe I ever thought my sweet and crazy aunt could ever murder a man in cold blood.

"It's beautiful." I migrate to her side so I can get a better look. My hand flutters to my chest. "It's got your three names! Oh, and I love this swirly pink design around the whole thing. Wow! You really got a tattoo?" The script isn't too hard to read, but the calligraphy is still quite dignified.

Winifred looks at her two best friends. "I went and got mine done first. Karen is next, whenever she conjures up the courage."

Karen bats her hand at Winifred. "I'll do it, I'll do it."

Marianne grins, her hands clasped in a swoon. "You're getting matching tattoos? That's so cool!"

Karen stands and smacks her bony left buttock. "I'm getting mine right here. Give the tattoo artist something to dream about when he goes home."

It's exactly the hearty laugh I need, and I feel it down to my toes.

Karen sits back down and picks up her hand of cards. "I'll need ample recovery time, though, so feel free to wait on me round the clock. I plan on being a pain in the butt, since, you know, I'll have a pain on my butt."

Marianne and Agnes share a laugh, but something about Karen's phrasing sticks in my brain.

"You're right," I point out, making my way to the front door. "You shouldn't be alone while you're recovering." I meet Marianne's gaze. "And we shouldn't have sent Helen home by herself. Does she have anyone there with her to make sure she's safe?"

"Safe?" Agnes echoes.

"Robert knows," Marianne points out, freezing as she puts the pieces together. "We were talking with Helen about him being there the night of the murder, which conflicted with what he told the police. Robert came into the kitchen in the middle of the conversation. If he suspects Helen went to the police..."

I'm already pushing my feet into my heels. "Without Helen's testimony to put him with his father and undo his lies, there is nothing substantial sticking him to the crime."

Marianne is right behind me, grabbing up her keys. "I'll drive."

I spin around and point at the three old women who

are coming toward us. "No way. You three stay here and bolt the door. I mean it. Don't open the door for anything. Got it?"

Agnes puts a hand on Winifred's shoulder and the other on Karen's, acting as the responsible adult. "Be safe, girls."

I dash out the front door and shut myself in the passenger's seat of Marianne's rickety beige sedan. I barely buckle myself in before she is flying down the road, a wild gleam in her eyes.

Marianne's worry comes out in a mess. "I can't believe we let Helen walk out of the precinct without going with her. She's a sweet person. If Robert does anything to her..."

I take a deep breath and do what I can to keep my cool. "For all we know, Sheriff Flowers has already arrested Robert."

"For all we know, he's dragging his heels on this, like he always does, giving Robert plenty of time to go after Helen."

My eyes close as I flinch at a flash of memory. "The sheriff told her to call in sick to work. Robert knows she's at home."

Marianne stomps harder on the gas, bypassing the speed limit until it is a mere suggestion to be batted away at will. Her car's engine roars as if it has not known oil in months.

I don't know the way or how long it will take, but I am certain we are already too late. I mentally prepare myself to see my second dead body since coming to the cute little town of Sweetwater Falls.

When Marianne peels into the driveway ten excruciating minutes later, she shouts at the blue coupe parked down the street. "That's Robert's car!"

I pull out my phone and call the police station, but Marianne is too determined to wait for the grownups with guns to get here. She bolts out of the car—my sweet librarian come to life—and tries to open the locked front door. The curtains of the big picture window are closed, even though it is the middle of the day, so we cannot see if there is peril inside.

The phone rings forever as I leap off the front porch and sprint after Marianne, knowing there is no scenario in which everything ends peacefully. "Around the back!"

She trips over an errant tree root, but I manage to catch her arm before she falls.

I am leading the way now as we race past the row of petunias. I zip around a few gardening tools along the side of the sweet little ranch-style home.

Finally, a person at the police station picks up. My words spill out in a rush. "Hello, send the Sheriff to Helen's house." When the dispatcher doesn't seem to grasp the severity of the situation, or even the case to which I am referring, I all but growl under my breath while I race to the backdoor.

"Locked!" Marianne moans.

My heart drops when I hear Helen's scream coming from inside the house.

I explain the situation to the person on the phone in as few clipped sentences as possible, and then end the call. Breathless, I cast around for anything that might look like a hide-a-key.

Marianne resorts to pounding her fists on the door. "Helen! Helen, you're not alone! We'll get you out!"

I don't know if some of Marianne's signature wildness is leaping onto me, or if my bravery has taken a turn for the worst. But as my feet move back the way we came, I don't hesitate to grab up the shovel that is propped on the side of the house.

I race to the porch, but I don't go for the door. It's been a hot minute since I've held a baseball bat, but even if my grip is wrong, my swing carries enough force from my adrenaline that I am certain I have just hit a home run.

The end of the shovel crashes into the glass, spidering the clean surface with the first blow.

The second blow sends a handful of shards into the front room of Helen's house.

I silently apologize when the third hit shatters enough of the window for me to climb through after I discard the shovel. My arm snags on a jagged edge, and my shin is sliced on a sharp shard, but I barely feel any of it.

Helen's scream fills the house, but I don't see her. I race down the hallway, realizing I made a wrong turn when her subsequent shout makes it clear she is in the basement.

I catch a flash of Marianne climbing through the window, shovel in hand in my periphery, but I don't slow. I take the steps to the basement three at a time, all but flying down to face the man who never learned to keep his childish tantrums under control.

"Helen!" I cry, racing toward my scared and bleeding friend in the corner.

I have no plan when Robert turns to face me, steak knife in hand. I recognize his weapon of choice, as it is the same utensil I used to make apple coleslaw alongside Helen when we first met.

I should have brought the shovel to use as a weapon.

I should have waited for the police.

I probably should have a better plan than to throw myself at Robert, foregoing the eminent danger of the knife clutched in his fist.

I missed my calling as a football player, apparently,

because Robert hits the concrete floor when I pummel him as hard as I can.

"Charlotte, careful!" Helen shouts.

Careful doesn't get the job done. I have been careful my whole life. I can't resign myself to a life lived carefully a moment longer.

I have to be brave.

Robert is strong, but I am in no mood to lose this fight. Years of pent-up frustration belts out of me. I refuse to play it safe for another second.

Robert rolls so he is on top of me, knife poised dangerously close to my cheek. "Perfect," he says, spitting through gritted teeth. "Save me the trip of having to track you down next."

There is no fear that hits me, only renewed determination. Gerald will be the only person to die at this man's hands.

This very day, his killer will be locked up.

The edge of the serrated knife drags along my cheek. My hand cups his wrist, holding it at bay as well as I am able. His strength is making mine seem laughable as my hand begins to shake under the effort of trying to keep him from cutting me.

I barely put together the actions of my sweet best friend in my periphery. There is true terror in her eyes as she raises up the shovel I had left on the porch. Her two braids fly out as brings the thing down on Robert's head with a sickening crack.

The man who believed in my cupcakes and took a chance on my business lets out a loud bray of agony, and then goes limp atop my supine body.

The knife drops from his grip, giving me the opportunity to escape from underneath his form.

Marianne has tears in her eyes. She looks equal parts terrified and livid as she holds the shovel in her hands. Marianne is trembling but still ready to repeat the punishment, should Robert rouse before the police get here.

I grab up the steak knife and crawl to Helen's side. She has a long gash on her forearm that has bled onto her pants and shirt.

"Oh, honey," I coo, my body quaking but still focused. I sit beside her and gather the woman into my arms, holding onto her with the knife clutched in my fist.

"He said he just wanted to talk," Helen blubbers, holding her arm. "I shouldn't have opened the door."

I shush her and hold her tighter. "You're safe now. We won't let him hurt you. He's going to jail, and you won't ever have to see his face again."

Marianne looks like a warrior, shovel at the ready. The only thing that startles her is when a cavalcade of footsteps rain down overhead. She calls up to retrieve the help that came just a little too late to get in on the action.

My arms are stiff around Helen, tensed so tightly that I cannot move them, even when Sheriff Flowers barrels down the steps toward us. He races to the scene, cuffing Robert, even though the man is still unconscious.

Marianne spills the details of the rescue in rushed, high-pitched sentences that smash together. Though she makes it through the entire explanation, I am not sure she has taken a single breath.

Two other officers are here, but I cannot tear my gaze from Robert. Though he is cuffed, my body will not believe it's over until he is dragged out of here and driven to the police station.

"Charlotte," comes a voice that nearly sends me into cardiac arrest.

Yet, even though the sound of Logan saying my name is distraction enough for most situations, I can't bring myself to look away from Robert. I can't unlock my arm from around Helen. I can't let go of the knife. My entire body is locked down, frozen as I struggle to compute how my time in Sweetwater Falls has led me here.

I don't answer Logan. I'm not sure I'm capable of speech just yet.

It's a struggle for Helen to wriggle out of my grip. The third officer has to help extract her from my tight hug. He is careful with Helen's trembling form as he guides her up the steps.

Robert rouses, as if sensing his prey has left the room.

I did not think it possible for me to reach a level of anxiety this acute. "Marianne! Hit him with the shovel again!" I cry.

Sheriff Flowers deftly arrests the shovel from Marianne. "I think I prefer my criminals alive. Makes them easier to get into the squad car so they can go to jail." When Marianne's chin firms in defiance, the sheriff cups her shoulder in a paternal manner. "I've got it from here. You did a great job, Marianne."

Marianne's lower lip quivers but she doesn't break down completely. Not yet. "I'll help you get him up the stairs."

Though Marianne is a slight thing, the sheriff doesn't turn down the help.

My body is still tucked into the corner of the basement, my knees pressed to my chest.

When Logan squats before me, my vision is filled with a

sight too perfect to belong on the backdrop of such a horrid day. My mouth pops open but no sound comes out when he strokes my cheek. The warmth of his touch lights my face with a blush that I am fairly certain will never go away.

Logan pulls his hand away and displays a finger streaked with red. "You're bleeding, Miss Charlotte. I'm guessing this knife thought you were a juicy steak?"

I know Logan is trying to be friendly and make a joke, but I can't understand it. Or I can't remember how normal people react to small niceties like that.

"I wrestled a knife away from Robert," I whisper.

Logan's expression turns grim. "That must have been frightening. Can you tell me where else you're hurt? I don't know which stains are your blood and which patches of red belong to Helen."

I am unable to feel much of my extremities. The terror is still coursing through me. "He had Helen cornered, so I tackled him."

Logan's lips press together. "That was so dangerous. I'm sorry we didn't get here sooner. You did the right thing, calling the station." His head dips down and he leans in. "Though, I would have preferred you wait for us, rather than break the window and have to wrestle a madman to the ground. Robert was armed and clearly ready to kill."

I blink at him, unable to formulate an intelligent response.

Logan seems to understand that I have hit my limit today. "How about I take this knife and put it somewhere safe. Would that be okay?"

I nod, but I can't relax my grip.

Again, Logan doesn't miss a beat. His touch is tender as he takes my hand between his, massaging my fingers. Finally, my fist unfurls, presenting him with the weapon used to assault poor Helen.

When the third officer comes back down, Logan hands him the knife to bag for evidence. Then he turns back to me, still squatting in my eyeline. "I think we should probably get you out of here. Can you stand?"

I blink at him, unsure if my legs possess the coordination or the strength to support my weight.

The compassion Logan fixes on me shows me a glimpse of why this man is so much more than a pretty face.

Logan rocks forward onto his knees and takes my wrists in his capable hands. "Let me help you up the stairs." He drapes my arms around his neck and then fixes his hands to my waist. In one deft motion, Logan lifts me until I am standing before him, though it's clear when I wobble that I am unsteady on my feet.

Logan glues my side to his, moving us both slowly

toward the stairs. We take each step together while he treats me to the perfection of his cologne.

He doesn't stop when we reach the top of the stairs, but rather he helps me through the house. He sets a slow pace as we move past the wreckage that is Helen's front window, and out into the afternoon sun.

Neighbors are gathered around, watching from across the street as Marianne folds her arms and glares into the backseat of the cop car. She is fierce and unapologetic.

I love it.

I, however, am on the verge of a total and complete breakdown.

My presence diverts Marianne's focus. She goes from tough woman to tender mother bear, dashing toward me. "She's cut up pretty bad," Logan informs her, though I wonder if he is exaggerating. I can't feel much, other than my acute anxiety.

"I'll get her to the doctor right now. Help me get her into my car?"

Marianne scampers to her beige sedan, starting up the spluttering engine while Logan lowers me into the passenger's seat. He even goes so far as to lean my seat back and buckle me in. "Expect the sheriff will be calling you both for a statement."

Marianne nods succinctly. "No problem."

Logan thumbs at my cheek, turning my head to face him more fully. His eyes are filled with concern, making him all the more breathtaking. "I'll check on you after we process Robert. No more solving crimes without me, got it?"

I manage a wan smile. "No promises."

Logan answers with an airy laugh before he backs away and shuts the door.

Marianne wastes no time putting distance between us and the scene of the crime, but my heart is still racing.

23

TWINKLE LIGHT MEMORIES

*N*ews of Robert's arrest and subsequent confession spread quickly through Sweetwater Falls. I have spent most days since his arrest waiting tables. Lately, the townspeople only frequent the diner to garner juicy details about Robert's culpability from me.

Bill, the owner, could not be happier to have my clumsy and unenthusiastic waitressing skills at his subpar establishment, because the diner has never been busier.

By the end of each shift, my plastered "Can I help you?" smile is cracked and broken beyond repair, peppered with exhaustion. It's a good thing I am booked for my one day off, helping hang twinkle lights for the festival tonight. I need a good distraction.

Time with Marianne is good for the soul. Not only is she incredibly organized (which, when you are in charge of hanging millions of tiny lights, is a must), but she also has a passion for the event. She has a clear vision of what she wants the night to feel like, and how each corner and crevice of the event should look.

My girl even has schematics.

The entire town square has been taken over by booths, a stage, an open area for dancing, and enough fair-like items that make it clear this town is no slouch at putting together events that spoil and celebrate its residents. The grassy field in the center of the city has a permanent stage set up with an awning overtop, which makes me think they have live music here on occasion.

Marianne put me in charge of lighting the area that has the photo booth, a pie stand, the punch booth, and a few other novelties that I cannot wait to experience.

It's a bad idea to perch atop a ladder that has been placed on uneven grass, but at this point, it's my only option. Marianne wants the photo booth to look just so, and darn it, that girl should have whatever she wants. I'm glad I'm not wearing my heels today. Jean shorts and a fitted pink t-shirt paired with purple gym shoes are the way to go when the day is spent hauling heavy boxes of twinkle lights and hanging them at odd (yet perfect) angles.

"It's amazing," Marianne comments from behind me. I nearly lose my balance, but manage to steady myself before I topple off the ladder.

I make quick work of hanging the last strand of lights for my area. I want Marianne to be able to inspect the finished product without having to imagine the rest into being.

"You're happy with it?" I ask, climbing down the ladder. When I turn to face her, I'm startled to find moisture sparkling on the apple of her cheek. "What's wrong?"

Marianne shakes her head and swipes at her cheek. "I knew you would get it just right. I wasn't expecting to feel all this, though." She motions to the photo booth. "That's where Jeremy proposed."

All tasks fly out of my head as I gather her in my arms. "I'm so sorry he hurt you. He's a fool."

Marianne lets a few soundless sobs loose on my shoulder but manages composure after half a minute. "It's all fine. Just stings sometimes when I see something like this. It's exactly how it was that night."

"Did you mean for that to happen?"

"I meant to follow the instructions set out. It's the same setup every year."

My mouth screws to the side. "Well, I can fix that. You get out of here. Go check on the other sections.

When you come back, I will make sure this corner doesn't look like a bad memory."

Marianne draws back in hesitation. "But we have to follow the instructions. It looks the same every year."

I smirk at her. "I guess that crazy city girl blew into town and mixed everything up."

Marianne giggles, rolls back her shoulders the second her tears dry, and then migrates to the next area.

Instead of horizontal lines, I unhook a few strands and layer them diagonal across the remaining parallel strings of lights. Then I beeline to the box of miscellaneous bows that have no assigned purpose, but were to be used to fill in missing or broken lights if needed. Instead of sporadic placement, I tie them to the edges of the photo booth, and up and down each corner. When I'm finished, the corner has been spattered with lines of bows instead of just the traditional twinkle lights. The whole thing look like a gigantic cake.

Or maybe everything looks like desserts to me.

Marianne blows her whistle, gathering all the volunteers to her. "Alright, everyone. Great work. People should be arriving in the next ten minutes, so let's get the boxes back on the flatbed. Paul is going to drive them to the town barn for storage. Any questions?"

One person with a raspy voice shouts out, "Did you really stab Robert to get him off of Helen?"

Another says, "I heard you and the new girl beat him almost to death to avenge Gerald."

Yet another chimes in with a helpful, "I heard Robert has a collection of knives that he uses to cook with and to kill with. Is that true?"

Marianne gapes at the volunteers, who clearly do not have the festival on their minds. "I don't think I want to talk about that right now. Does anyone have any questions *about the festival?*"

If there were crickets nearby, they would be chirping. It is clear that all anyone wants to talk about is the murder and the arrest.

Twilight is nearing, so it's almost showtime.

Marianne clicks her pen. "Alright, then. Thank you for your help. The vendors are ready, the teardown team has a healthy amount of volunteers, so your only job now is to enjoy the festival." She dons a cheery grin, which communicates to the team that she will not tolerate talk about her propensity to beat people over the head with a shovel to save her friend.

Some things get to stay between us.

When the townspeople begin to filter in, I am enamored of their excitement and curiosity. Though it's clear this event never changes from year to year, the whole thing is new to me.

It seems the residents of Sweetwater Falls have not

lost their knack for viewing the world with childlike wonder. As people filter in, they gape at the beauty, marveling with their mouths dropped open as they point at various displays.

My eyes search until I find Winifred, Karen and Agnes. Karen is arguing with Amos Vandermuth, both of them using wild hand gestures and sarcastic head swivels.

I will never keep up with these three.

"You're a cheapskate, Amos!" Karen doesn't bother to keep their conversation private by invoking a respectable volume. She clutches her knitting bag to her chest as she yells at him.

"I'm a taxpayer!" His angled finger rises sanctimoniously. "I've already paid for this event by paying my taxes. I shouldn't have to pay an entrance fee when my money went into helping create this whole thing!" He motions wildly to the festival at large.

Winifred snarls at him, arms akimbo. "Every single year we have this same stinking argument. Who did you swindle into letting you in for free this year?"

Amos lifts his long nose. "I pay every year with the money they take from my taxes!"

Agnes throws up her hands and stomps off. "I can't with you. I just can't." Her eyes land on me and her entire expression changes. "Hi, honey. This festival is spectacular. Best one yet. Well done!" She wraps her arms around me and kisses my cheek with her soft lips.

"It's kind of amazing, isn't it? Marianne is a visionary."

"She sure is. I..." Agnes' sentence falls when her gaze lights on the photo booth across the way. "Oh, she changed it! Thank goodness." She calls over her shoulder. "Karen, stand down. We don't need your knitting bag."

I raise my brow. "You were planning on knitting in the photo booth? I can take a picture of you doing that now, if you like."

Agnes waves off my confusion. "No, no. That booth has been breaking Marianne's heart for the past few years. We were going to take care of it. But maybe now that it looks so different, she'll be okay."

I cross my arms over my chest. "I redecorated that corner, so it doesn't look like it did when she got her photo taken when Jeremy proposed. Marianne seemed relieved, so hopefully she's not too wounded tonight." My brain catches on Agnes' phrasing. "What do you mean, you were going to 'take care of it?'"

Karen comes over and opens her knitting bag. Instead of yarn, I gasp when inside her bag are matches, a bottle of liquor and an old newspaper. "Guess we don't need these, then."

Winifred sighs. "Shame. The one thing missing from this festival is fireworks."

I draw myself up and fix them with the best scold I can muster, hoping it hides my shock. "Give me that. You three don't need to go committing more crimes."

"What's that about committing crimes?" comes a voice I truly cannot handle right now.

Or ever, come to think of it.

"Logan," I say, breathless at the sight of him. Jeans and a green button up over a t-shirt make him look like a model for, well, just about everything. Whatever he's selling, I'm sure I would buy it.

"How are you feeling, Miss Charlotte?" His gaze drifts to the cut on my cheek. It didn't require stitches, but the two-inch scab is still visible.

Though, if he can even see the mark beneath my blush, I will be quite surprised.

I touch the nape of my neck, noting the sudden heat that floods my body. "Oh, fine." I dip my head and turn my body partly from Karen, Agnes and Winifred, who are smirking at me knowingly. "Hey, thank you for helping me to the car the other day."

"You shouldn't thank me," Logan says, the corner of his mouth lifting with a tender tease. "You should be angry that I didn't take you to get medical attention myself. Marianne was so ferocious that she take care of you that I didn't step in. But I should have." He points to a booth where you can try your luck throwing rings around milk bottle tops in hopes of winning a live goldfish. "Let me make it up to you?"

I freeze up, my brows shooting skyward. "What?"

"She would love to," Winifred offers, while Karen nudges me toward him.

Agnes points to his side. "A gentleman would offer his arm to escort her."

If I could be more embarrassed, I would disintegrate into the grass, I'm sure. "That's really not necessary."

Logan trains his beautiful, bright green orbs on me, rendering me helpless. "Please?"

I dip my chin and lean toward him, hoping to keep my chagrin private. "You know how I get around you. Are you sure this is a good idea?"

Logan's self-satisfied smirk tells me he loves teasing me very much. "I think we're safe. It would be another thing if I was taking you to throw darts. That could turn hazardous." He taps the toe of his shoe to mine, looking on the verge of shy as he shoves his hands in his pockets. "Let me win you a goldfish?"

Before I can say "Yes," "Are you sure?" pops out.

Logan proffers his arm to me, his chest swelling like a man on a mission. "Very."

Winifred's palm finds its way to the small of my

back. "Be brave," she reminds me.

And suddenly, my feet find themselves clearing the small gap between us. My anxiety spikes as I hold on to Logan's arm. I can only hope my most harrowing days are behind me.

Logan and I walk through the ceiling of twinkle lights, under the bright glow of Sweetwater Falls' rising moon.

"Murder aside, are you glad you came to Sweetwater Falls?" he asks me as we approach the ring toss booth.

I take a chance and blink up at him, noting that his stunning features only look more heroic and noble when illuminated by twinkle lights. "Murder aside, Sweetwater Falls just might be my new favorite place."

I have never belonged anywhere. Not really. But as Logan pays for two rounds of ring tossing, I realize that, surrounded by these cooky townspeople and all of their quirks, I just might have found my true home.

The End

Love the book?
Leave a review.

24

VANILLA CARDAMOM CUPCAKE

From the cozy mystery novel *Vanilla Vengeance*
by Molly Maple

"*It's a vanilla bean cupcake with a vanilla bean cardamom glaze, topped with Italian meringue that was made with vanilla bean and cardamom sugar.*"

-*Vanilla Vengeance*

INGREDIENTS FOR THE CUPCAKE:
1¼ cups all-purpose flour

1¼ tsp baking powder

½ tsp salt

½ cup unsalted butter, softened

¾ cup granulated sugar

2 large eggs, room temperature

1 tsp pure vanilla extract

1 vanilla pod, divided

½ cup buttermilk, plain yogurt or vanilla yogurt, room temperature

INSTRUCTIONS FOR THE CUPCAKE:

1. Preheat the oven to 350°F and line a cupcake pan with cupcake liners.
2. In a medium bowl, sift together 1¼ cups flour, 1¼ tsp baking powder, and ½ tsp salt. Set flour mix aside.
3. In a large bowl, use a mixer to beat the butter and sugar on medium speed for three minutes. Beat until shiny, scraping down the sides of the bowl as needed.
4. Take your vanilla pod and split it lengthwise down the center with a paring knife. Then take your knife and scrape the seeds from the middle. Add half the pod's worth of seeds

into the butter mixture. Reserve the other half for the frosting and glaze.

5. Add eggs one at a time while the mixer runs on low speed. Add 1 tsp pure vanilla extract. Mix until smooth.

6. With the mixer on low speed, add the flour mixture in thirds, alternating with the yogurt. Mix to incorporate with each addition, scraping down the sides of the bowl as needed. Beat until just combined.

7. Divide the batter into your 12-count lined cupcake pan, filling each one 2/3 the way full.

8. Bake for 20-24 minutes at 350°F, or until a toothpick stuck in the center comes out clean.

9. Let them cool in the pan for 10 minutes, then transfer to a cooling rack. Cool to room temperature before frosting.

INGREDIENTS FOR THE GLAZE:

Less than ½ cup water

2½ cups white sugar

13 cardamom pods

The other half of the vanilla pod

. . .

INSTRUCTIONS FOR THE GLAZE:

1. Take the other half of the vanilla pod and scrape the seeds into your food processor.
2. Shell your cardamom pods easily by lying them flat on your cutting board, laying your knife atop them, and smacking the flat of the blade with your fist. The pods will crack, exposing the rows of seeds inside when you open the pods. Add the seeds (not the shells) to the food processor.
3. Pulse the two ingredients together until the pods are broken to a powder.
4. Add the white sugar to the food processor and pulse a few times, making sure not to overmix. You do not want this to become powdered sugar yet.
5. Take out 1½ cups of the perfumed sugar and set aside for the frosting.
6. Now pulse the remaining sugar mixture in your food processor until the perfumed white sugar becomes powdered sugar.
7. Sift the processed powdered sugar into a small mixing bowl. Going slowly, add water

two teaspoons at a time, mixing with a
spatula until your desired glaze consistency
forms.

8. Dip the tops of your cooled cupcakes into the
glaze, or drizzle over top. Then set back on
the wire rack to cool.

Ingredients for the Frosting:

1½ cups of your vanilla cardamom sugar

1/3 cup water

5 egg whites

½ tsp cream of tartar

Instructions for the Frosting:

1. Combine your 1½ cups of perfumed sugar
mixture in a medium saucepan with 1/3 cup
of water. Over medium heat, stir steadily
until the sugar dissolves, forming a glassy
glaze (it should reach 240°F).

2. In a clean, dry, large mixing bowl, whip your
5 egg whites with ½ tsp cream of tartar on
medium speed until soft peaks form.

3. In a steady stream while the mixer is on high speed, pour the sugar glaze down the side of the bowl. The meringue should still be warm while holding its shape. Whip until you reach your desired consistency (usually somewhere between soft peaks and stiff peaks).

4. Place a dollop of the Italian meringue on your cooled cupcake and serve.

MARSHMALLOW MURDER

Enjoy a free preview of *Marshmallow Murder*,
book two in the Cupcake Crimes series.

Marshmallow Murder

It's not easy being new to a town as small and close-knit as Sweetwater Falls. But in the few months I have lived here, I am lucky enough to have made some truly fantastic friends. Coming from a big city where everything moved fast and didn't stick around long, life in Sweetwater Falls is a welcome change of pace.

Though, I did not foresee stumbling onto a dead body my first day in town.

I am new at most things around here, but as I flip the menu over and scrub it down, it is clear to me that waiting tables will always be old hat.

Bill's Diner isn't exactly what anyone would consider fine dining, but a waitressing job pays what little bills I have, so I can't complain too much. It shouldn't matter that this place isn't my dream. I'm sure most people don't work a job that makes them come alive. The oldies music playing over the loudspeaker does the opposite of putting pep in my step.

But I swear, every time I serve a piece of pie that tastes like the box it was shipped here in, a little part of my soul dies. For one brief week, I had an arrangement with the Spaghetti Scarf restaurant. But after the debacle I was involved in with the previous owner—finding him dead and then getting far too deep into solving his murder—I have been informed my culinary services are no longer needed.

I am a baker, as I have told Bill several times before. But he is not interested in my baking skills, only my waitressing ability.

The fact that it is dead in here this morning doesn't exactly inspire confidence in the current menu. This place looks straight out of the fifties, complete with a juke box in the corner. The booths are always in need of a wipe down, but no matter how many times I scrub them clean, the restaurant always looks worn and outdated.

Bill comes out of the kitchen, wiping his hands on a once-white towel. He tucks it into the apron that's cinched around his pooched belly. Bill glances around the diner and sighs. "It's the summer slump. Everyone is outside doing outdoor things."

"Maybe if you fixed the air conditioning, people would stay longer while they eat." It's meant to be said as a legitimate suggestion, but the way I mumble it makes me sound like I am being passive-aggressive.

Bill raises a bushy eyebrow at me but doesn't comment on my feedback. When the phone rings, he doesn't move to answer it. He stares me down until I pick up the receiver.

I guess when the hostess is sent home early, the only waitress on the clock is supposed to answer the phones. "Bill's Diner," I say, trying to sound chipper and inviting.

"I'd like to order a burger and fries to..." The person with a muffled voice rattles off the address.

"Sure thing. Would you like to add a side of apple-sauce for a dollar?" I hate upselling. It makes me feel dirty. But Bill insists we do it, and he is currently standing within earshot.

"That's fine. What's the name on the order?"

"Amos Vandermuth."

I smile, grateful whenever I hear a name I know. "Oh, hi, Amos. It's Charlotte. How are you? You sound like you're coming down with a cold or something."

"Huh? I'm fine. I'll pay when you get here."

I'll bet you will. The man likes to argue over every penny that passes through his crooked fingers. Just last month, he was haggling over the two-dollar entry ticket to the Twinkle Lights Festival, claiming he shouldn't have to pay anything, since his tax dollars go to the town anyway.

I mean, honestly.

I put in the order to Bill, who shuffles his feet when he walks back into the kitchen, no doubt wishing for a larger party.

When the front door chimes, Bill zips back out, hopeful that more customers have forsaken the outdoors so they can sweat in here. "Oh. You. You're ordering something, right?" His skin is reddened—from the heat or from his natural coloring, I'm never quite sure.

My best friend shoots Bill a wry look. "I'm here on my break to see your best waitress. I'll have a strawberry milkshake and two straws."

I grin at Marianne, grateful to see her face. She's tugging on one of her two brown braids, which I know means she's thinking hard about something.

"I'm taking my break, Bill!" I tear off my apron and scamper to our favorite booth—the one in the far corner that smells least of French fry oil. Though, no matter how hard I try to steer clear of the stench, I always have to dart into the shower the second I get home.

I love that my Aunt Winifred's house has started to feel like a home to me.

Marianne slides into our usual booth of choice, her shoulders slumped.

"What's got you down, babe?" I ask, my elbows propped on the table.

"The library needs more funding to update our catalog, but of course, there's no money in the city's budget for it. The library doesn't get enough traffic coming in and out, they say, so they can't increase the budget to get new books. It's either fix the leak in the roof or buy new books." She tilts her chin back to let out a loud, exasperated moan. "Of course, with no new books this year at all, why would anyone come in? Not everyone loves the classics as much as I do."

No one loves the classics as much as Marianne. She always carries a book in her purse to read in her down time.

"I'm sorry to hear that." I take in the slumped nature of her petite frame. "Who can we harass to make this happen?"

"The town selectman isn't exactly open to suggestions on how he should spend the town's budget. At least that's what he told me when I tried yesterday."

My mouth pulls to the side in a frown. "Is this something we should stick the Live Forever Club on? Aunt Winifred, Karen and Agnes don't exactly take no for an answer."

Our favorite elderly ladies have a penchant for causing the best kind of trouble.

"They are busy putting together their roulette tournament. I don't want to bother them about books." The way she says it makes it sound like she is losing some of her passion for her favorite escape.

I reach across the table and place my hand atop hers. "You aren't bothering anybody ever. What's going on? This isn't you."

Though I have only known her for a few months, I feel confident in claiming that truth aloud.

She rests her forehead atop the table. "I was hoping to buy all the books on the community center ladies' book club list. The As the Page Turns club members are always asking for the year's newest releases."

"That's really the book club's name? That's cute."

"I love that they make it such a priority to read. To not be able to do this one thing for them feels like I let down the entire town. But there literally isn't any room in the budget."

"It's not your fault," I remind her, squeezing her wrist.

"I am the head librarian. It has to be someone's fault. The buck stops with me. I can be frustrated with the town selectman, sure, but maybe I didn't push hard enough. Maybe I didn't budget well enough." She picks her head up, only to bang it over and over on the table-top. "I know that's not it. Not a penny gets wasted. I had Amos Vandermuth go over my books again just last week to see if we could squeeze any additional funds that might have been misspent."

I chuckle at the idea of the old, crotchety miser sitting down with the spunky librarian while they pour over ledgers. "Did he have any good insight?" I place my hand over her head, so she stops banging it.

Marianne picks up her head but keeps her chin low to the table. "My budget passed the Vandermuth test, so I know it's solid. The money just isn't there, and it isn't coming."

My lips purse as I share in her frustration. "We'll think of something."

Bill calls from the back. "Carryout order up!"

I narrow my eyes at his form that peeks out through the half window. "I'm on break, and I'm not your delivery girl. I'm your waitress."

Bill points at me with a dirty wooden spoon. "You're my carryout girl until we get some hungry customers in here. Address is on the bag."

"Speak of the devil," I murmur. "Feel like going on a delivery with me?"

Marianne sits up. Her olive skin is slightly rosy in the center of the forehead where she was banging it on the tabletop. "Sure. If you feel like replacing the radio on your drive with my whining."

"Music to my ears." I grab up the carryout bag, my purse and her milkshake to go.

The sunshine is warm and welcoming, if not a little too hot as we step outside. There is no breeze, so the air is stagnant and soupy. Still, I don't mind the discomfort because I love the sunshine on my skin. I can practically feel the vitamin D soaking into my pours, lifting my spirits as natural happiness is supposed to do. Enough sunshine, and maybe my blonde hair will lighten a few shades naturally.

Marianne remains glum, but she still makes for good company while we drive the eight minutes to Amos Vandermuth's home.

I have never been here before, but the one-story abode couldn't possibly belong to anyone else. The tall man in his seventies has a hooked nose and a scowl that I'm guessing he was born wearing. His brown cardigan was ratty and unkempt when I saw him last, and his lawn matches perfectly.

I kinda like the guy, angry though he always is. Marianne is closer to him, though. She tolerates his gruff, miser ways better than most.

I am not expecting a tip on this order. I'll be lucky if he pays for it without a fight.

Marianne is my shadow as I trot to the front door and ring the bell, which of course, doesn't work. The porch is cracked. The gray shutter is hanging at an odd angle. The window is opened and flies are filtering in and out like they are frequenting an all you can eat buffet.

"I hate that he lives like this," Marianne comments, though not with an ounce of judgment, only compassion. "I came over last week to help him get his garbage can out of the garage because it had fallen over and he couldn't manage it. Didn't look much better then."

No one comes to the door, but I don't fidget too much while we wait. I figure when I am in my seventies, I will need people to be patient with me getting anywhere.

Marianne curls one of my blonde locks around her finger, seeing if she can make it spiral without a hot iron. "Do you think he forgot he ordered food?"

I shrug and ring the doorbell again. "I would just leave it, but he didn't pay. He said he would pay when I dropped it off."

When it is clear no one is coming, yet his golf cart is in the driveway, Marianne reaches out and turns the knob.

"What?" she asks of my scandalized gasp. "No one

locks their doors in Sweetwater Falls. It's a very safe town."

"Right. Where the only people breaking in are librarians."

"I'm just checking on him." She opens the door and cranes her neck inside. "Amos? Amos, it's Marianne. Are you alright?"

I lean forward too, because in my mind, I am not officially breaking and entering if the door isn't locked, and I don't actually step a toe inside.

I'm not sure how solid my logic is, but that caution is overridden when a pungent stench hits my nose. "Oh, what is that?"

Marianne gags. "I don't know. His trash isn't that old. I just took it out for him last week."

"Maybe his refrigerator broke." Amos is the type to not replace a broken appliance even if his house smells like rotting garbage. Spending money is worse than a bad stench in his mind.

Marianne calls his name twice before the flies find us. There is a buzzing coming from the back of the house. Apparently, Marianne takes that as an invitation to come inside. "Amos, it's me. Are you alright?"

She veers away from the flies and goes toward the room to the left, which I am guessing is the bedroom.

I, however, am too curious not to investigate the source of the horrid smell.

I call out his name once more before my footsteps falter and then come to a stupefied stop.

"Marianne!" I mean to shout for my best friend, but my voice loses all sound. Over and over, I say her name, hoping she will come in here and tell me that what I am seeing cannot possibly be real.

I'm cold all over, frightened because there is no way to undo what has been done.

The flies have found their feast, alright, but not in a broken fridge.

Marianne screams when she enters the kitchen. She has more optimism than me, because she darts to his side and fishes for a pulse.

I can tell just by looking that Amos died a while ago.

From the looks of things, Amos Vandermuth has been dead for days.

"No, no, no..." Marianne repeats herself on a loop. She is no doubt in shock that anything so horrible could be possible in the small town utopia that is Sweetwater Falls.

Marianne's hand cups her mouth, her eyes flicking over Amos' sprawled form.

I take in the details at the slow pace my brain is able to process them.

There's a bowl of oatmeal spilled and dried on the kitchen floor.

A glass is broken, the shards scattered near the stove.

A chair is tipped to the side, while the other has been scooted out from the narrow table.

The yellowed and unwashed curtain that should be over the sink has been torn down.

I know I shouldn't, but I take out my phone and snap a few pictures. I get one of the body, sure, but I focus mostly on the chaos surrounding Amos.

Amos' head is bent to the left, his eyes open in frozen horror. His mouth is open, telling me he probably died pleading for either mercy or help.

My stomach sinks as I call the emergency help line.

It is clear to me that Amos did not die peacefully.

Read *Marshmallow Murder* today!

ABOUT THE AUTHOR

Author Molly Maple believes in the magic of hot tea
and the romance of rainy days.

She is a fan of all desserts, but cupcakes have a special
place in her heart. Molly spends her days searching for
fresh air, and her evenings reading in front of a
fireplace.

Molly Maple is a pen name for USA Today bestselling
fantasy author Mary E. Twomey, and contemporary
romance author Tuesday Embers.

Visit her online at www.MollyMapleMysteries.com.
Sign up for her newsletter to be alerted when her next
new release is coming.

Made in the USA
Las Vegas, NV
30 September 2021